AMERICA

~ A wild new land in the making ~

Indian, western and other short stories

By

Rick Magers

ALL RIGHTS RESERVED

© April 2007

No part of this book may be reproduced,
stored in a retrieval system, or transmitted
by any means, electrical, mechanical,
photocopying, recording, or otherwise,
without the written permission from the author.

The author appreciates feedback — magersrick@yahoo.com

Rick Magers

TABLE OF CONTENTS

Story   page

1.   Fair Dinkum Cobber----------------------4

2.   Buffalo and Men-----------------------35

3.   Woo Lee Chong-------------------------43

4.   The Lone Ranger-----------------------52

5.   Trouble in Sundance-------------------74

6.   Mysterious Gringo---------------------80

7.   Highpockets Dandy---------------------93

8.   Black Warrior-----------------------104

9.   Glyn MacCrimmon & The Apache--------133

10. Seminole----------------------------142

Rick Magers

1

FAIR DINKUM COBBER

The last man clomped down the gangplank in trail-worn boots into Yerba Buena, soon to be re-named San Francisco. He was short, deeply tanned, and looked as if God had used a pickle barrel as a model when designing his upper half. He wore suspenders to hold up his short pants, into which a heavy, plain, gray shirt was stuffed, and carried only a sack made of heavy broadcloth. His gray eyes scanned the wharf as he came down, apparently hoping to see someone awaiting his arrival. A soft floppy hat hung on the back of his neck from a rawhide tong, secured by a device holding a beautiful blue stone, from which many different colors radiated as the sun struck it. He stopped at the bottom, placed the sack at his feet and pulled the hat up, placing it over his rusty colored hair. After sliding the sparkling stone up beneath his square jaw, he retrieved the sack and headed toward the huge wooden building where most of the male passengers from the ship had gone. He paused after reaching it, put the sack once again on the ground, and removed the makings for a smoke.

Three men sat on the wide porch in front of him, silently watching. He deftly rolled a cigarette between two fingers and licked the paper. After returning the leather pouch of tobacco to his heavy shirt's pocket, he opened a small leather pouch and removed a single match.

Rick Magers

Returning the pouch to the pocket of his short leather pants, he lifted his leg slightly to tighten the shorts and pulled the match across his left buttock. None of the three men watching noticed that everything the oddly dressed stranger from the sailing vessel did was with his left hand. The right hand was never occupied, and always remained but a short reach from the huge knife hanging on his hip. It was the type of error that caused careless men to die.

He glanced up and read the sign to himself. *Fenster & Bullock—Supplies & Liquor. Yep! This's the place Moss mentioned in his letter.* He grabbed the sack, slung it over his left shoulder and walked up the six steps to the porch. The three men all noticed his odd footwear, but only the very old one on the end commented. "Them're nice boots y'got there, fella, but I ain't ever seen any like 'em. Where'd you get boots like that?"

He stepped aside and rested his sack on the porch as he leaned against the post. The smile that came across his face was warm and friendly, but had a hard, deep, penetrating directness to it. It made men feel at ease when they should have been cautious. Careless men with ill intent seldom had the opportunity to correct their errors when confronting him. "My Abo mate made 'em for me." His smile widened, "Made these bloody pants too 'e did. Best bloody fella I ever saw with a thread n' needle workin' on roohide."

"What kinda hide?" The old man leaned forward, and the other two leaned out to look.

"Roo…kangaroo. Best bloody critter there is to make bush clothes from."

"I heard of 'em," the old man commented, "kinda like a cow'r som'n ain't they?"

"Yeah! Sorta…I reckon." He smiled, and then asked, "You fellas sit 'ere often watchin' the people comin' in on the boats?"

"Yep!" The man in the middle answered, "We own a chunk of this place," he nodded toward the front door, "so that's all we do now, just watch the folks comin' to Yerba Buena to get rich catchin' beavers." His weatherworn old face opened to reveal a toothless grin.

"Elmo makes it sound like we're rich," the man on the far end said, "but we ain't."

"We pooled our money," the original talker said, "and bought a fifth of this place with Jim Fenster and Brady Bullock. We ain't rich n' ain't gonna git rich, but we don't hafta go trapping up in them mountains any more." He pointed toward the mountains to the north of what would become San Francisco in a few years. "Gits awful cold up there for old guys like us, and we get enough outa this deal to keep eatin' plus we got us a shack t'live in out behind the place." He grinned at the stranger, showing his two remaining teeth, "All we gotta do is clean up the place at night after they close 'er down."

"Not a bad deal I reckon, mates. Tell me som'n, did you see a bloke 'alf again as big's me with bright red hair, comin' through 'ere about a year ago?"

"Hmmmmm!" The man on the end rubbed his chin as his brow furrowed, "Did he have a little dog with him?"

The stranger's face lit up, "Bloody well did, mate. Small little terrier that would dance on 'is hind feet for any small treat of tucker."

"Of what?" the toothless man asked.

"Tucker," he looked at them each, and then motioned toward his mouth saying, "tucker, food, som'n to eat."

"Oh, never heard grub called that."

"Yeah," the man in the middle said, "he talked funny like you do, and said he was from some island way out yonder." His arthritic old forefinger pointed west at the Pacific Ocean.

"Australia, mate and she's no bloody island; she's a vast country 'at's fillin' up so fast that there'll be standin' room only soon…too soon t'suit me."

"Yeah! That's what he called it," the old man on the end said, "awstrailyer. Stayed around here for a week'r so then tied up with two fellers from Canadee. He lived n' trapped with the Flathead Injuns up yonder," he nodded toward the mountains. "Friend o' yours?"

"'E's me cobber n' Moss O'Rourke's 'is name." He nodded to each of the old men, but they looked at each other, and then at him; each with a questioning look on their face. "Cobber?" one said.

He looked from one to the other. "Your fair dinkum cobber is your best friend, and 'e'll do whatever 'e's gotta do to help you out. At least that's the way it is in Australia, mates." He smiled at each and extended his hand to the closest man. "Chaddy O'Shea's me name n' that's why I'm 'ere; ain't 'eard a bloody word from Moss but one time n' that was just after 'e landed 'ere. I thank you for tellin' me that y've seen 'im. Did 'e return here or stay up in the mountains?"

Rick Magers

"Come back down twice, they did," the toothless one said as he nodded his nearly bald head. "The last time he came, he was with both them fellers, and they had some gold what they'd found up there."

"Gold?" A frown crossed Chaddy's face. "Did they 'ave a lot or just a few nuggets?"

"Only a bit of panning dust and a few small nuggets." The man on the far end leaned forward, resting his arms on his knees, "One o' then Canadee fellers showed me his and it wasn't a bunch, but it was dern sure gold."

"They all three go back up in the mountains, did they?"

"Sure did," the end man answered after filling his mouth with tobacco, "stayed here long enough t'git some diggin' gear and a mule, then headed back up. Lemme see," he rubbed his chin as he worked the tobacco into position, and thought a moment. "that was back while it was still warm and it's now November," he looked around at his two friends, "ain't it?" They both nodded so he turned back to Chaddy, "Reckon that was about six months ago."

"Did they say where they were 'eaded?" Chaddy was excited to hear about his friend so soon after getting off the boat from Sydney.

The man on the far end spoke again. "The Canadee feller said they was gonna stop near that big ole mill some feller's buildin' up in them mountains, then they was gonna head on up n' keep trappin' with them Flatheads." He leaned out to ask his friend on the other end, "You's up there in forty-three, Homer, what's the name o' that place?"

"Sutter's Mill, and it wasn't in forty-three, it was the summer of forty-four; three years ago."

"Did my cobber and the blokes with 'im say any more about the gold?"

The old man chewing the tobacco answered after spitting on the ground. "Said they was gonna get enough beaver to buy supplies n' tools, then come back n' work their claim."

Chaddy looked hard at the man on the end, and figured him to be okay. "Homer, I'll get us a bottle o' good whiskey if you'll draw me a map to get me near that Sutter place." He grinned warmly at the old man and his friends, "Whadaya say, mates?"

The man stood, followed by his friends. "I'd say that you've hired yerself a map maker Cha, Chap, Channy," he stopped abruptly, "what was yer name?"

"Chaddy mate, Chaddy O'Shea."

Rick Magers

"Funny name."

"So's Homer, mate."

Homer grinned, "Name don't mean nothin' nohow," his grin widened, "specially when the guy wearin' it's buying the likker."

The three old men followed Chaddy into the trading post, then limped toward the rear when he said, "Get us a table mates, and I'll bring us a jug n' some paper for you to draw me that map on." He paid no particular attention to any of the men, moving back and forth in the vicinity of the long wooden bar, as he waited to buy the whiskey and a sheet of paper.

One man, however, had been paying close attention to him. He hadn't taken his eyes off the man in short pants since he entered with the three old locals. He was a huge, very dark complexioned man with unsmiling eyes that were as black as his hair and beard, which covered nearly his entire head and face. He was known only as Frenchy, and carried two of the recently manufactured Chatellerault single shot service pistols; both shoved down into a wide leather belt around his enormous belly. Soldiers of the French Army, from which he had earlier departed, also carried the new weapon.

His exit from France was hastily made at night, just after killing two men who had bested him in a game of cards. His losses and their moneybelts went with him to the coast in search of a sailing vessel to carry him away from France—and the executioner. He was a cowardly man, but dangerous when the odds were in his favor. Several men had died from his gunfire…always from the dark…always unexpected—always in the back.

Frenchy was just the kind of man that Jim Fenster and Brady Bullock had been looking for. They needed an unscrupulous man to assist them in their plans to dominate the waterfront area of the booming little settlement of Yerba Buena.

He sipped his wine and silently watched as Chaddy ordered a crock jug of whiskey; saying to the clerk behind the bar, "none o' last night's hog likker mate, or you'll get it back up side your head." His hard eyes fastened on the young man, "Good whiskey n' go ahead and charge me a fair price for it." After the young man assured him that he was getting the very best they had to offer, Chaddy asked him for a sheet of paper and a pencil. Frenchy's eyes narrowed as he watched the short stocky man head toward the table where the three old men sat waiting. *I wonder what he wants that paper for?*

Rick Magers

Homer took the sheet of coarse paper from Chaddy and laid it between him and his toothless friend Joshua, that Chaddy learned was the man's name. He asked and was told that the other old man's name was Elmo. Homer shoved the pencil into his thick gray beard and pulled the jug toward him. The three-finger-tall whiskey glasses from the previous group that used the table were still there, so the old man poured four of them to the brim. When the cork was back in the jug, he lifted his glass. "To your friend finding more of that gold and you finding your cobbler."

"She'll be right mate." Chaddy grinned wide and tossed the strong, month-old, artificially colored, amber liquor down. He shook his head slowly up and down before commenting, "Bloody good likker that is, by cracky."

Homer opened the jug and poured them all another. "Better'n it used t'be; that's fer dang sure. Brady Bullock hired a guy from Canadee that made regular likker in a likker factory up there. They sold s'dern much of it that the Canadee feller went back up n' brought back two more guys from that factory to work with him."

Chaddy sipped a little before speaking, "Let's get that map drawn before we get too close to the bottom o' the jug, mate."

Homer tossed his drink down then grinned, "Dern near forgot what we was sittin' here for."

During a half-hour of thinking and drawing, Homer filled his glass three times as Chaddy sipped on his first. The other two men accepted a new glassful each time Homer refilled his. "Okay," he said, finally satisfied that he had the map correct. "Pull your chair over next to me n' I'll explain where yer heading."

Completely un-noticed by everyone…except Chaddy, Frenchy had slowly worked his way to one of the huge wooden pillars that held up the roof. It was directly behind Elmo and was so large that the Frenchman had been leaning unseen…almost, against it listening, as he sipped his pint mug of wine. While he was waiting at the bar, Chaddy had seen something in the man's eyes that alerted him. He had spent ten years in Northern Australia, killing and skinning giant crocodiles to sell to the trading ships supplying the hide market in Paris France. Many of the ferocious beasts had attempted to sneak up on him, and all failed—just as this huge man had.

As Homer shoved the map over so it would be between him and Chaddy, Frenchy stepped out and placed his hand on it. "What do we have here, old man?" The last word no sooner fell from his thick, gluttonous lips, than it was replaced by a loud scream. The back of Chaddy's huge knife had landed right in the middle of Frenchy's hand.

Chaddy then brought the blade up against the side of Frenchy's big, dark head. As big as he was, Frenchy's head was no match for the wide side of Chaddy's blade, which was seventeen inches long and three inches wide at the widest place. His lights were out before he hit the floor. The bruised flesh on the back of his hand, where the blunt back edge of the knife had landed, was causing the hand to swell.

The older bartender heard the noise and came to the table. He looked down at the man who was not liked by him or anyone else, then asked, "What happened?"

"Dunno," Chaddy responded with a brief glance down, "pow," he snapped his fingers, "standin' 'er one bloody minute, then on the floor the next," he shook his head slightly, "'eart attack, I reckon."

The bartender looked at the hand that was now swollen to the size of a small melon. "Yeah, probably so." He turned toward the bar and called for the younger man to come and help him. When the boy arrived, the older man gave him instructions. "Let's drag him into the storeroom, and then you go get somebody to bring a wagon and take him to doc so he can have a look at him."

Chaddy watched as they each took a leg, and with effort, dragged Frenchy away. He turned back to Homer, "now let's get on about this bloody map." All three of the old men had remained silent since the huge knife flashed and came down on Frenchy's hand. Homer's hand shook a bit as he poured them each another glass of whiskey. He bolted his down then pointed at a spot on the map. "This's where you are now," he moved his finger to a spot northeast, "this's the area where your friend said they found that gold." He moved his finger north. "This's where them Flathead injuns they was trappin' beavers with, got 'em a big camp."

"High in them Seeairy Nevaders," Joshua grinned; his toothless mouth lopsided, and his blurry, drunken eyes glazed. "Been there m'self back when ole Joe Walker brought his exdeepeeshun, exedeeshun," he twisted his mouth a few time before giving up on the word, "buncha people in wagons across." Another grin and he brought the newly filled glass of whiskey toward his mouth, spilling half on the way.

Rick Magers

Chaddy spent just long enough with Homer to be certain that he understood the map, and then he stood. "Well mates, I've enjoyed me time with you, but I'm gonna get m'self an 'orse, some trail tucker n' supplies, then get on up there t'find me fair dinkum cobber." With a wave he turned and left the three men pouring themselves another glassful.

A few doors down from Fenster & Bullock's place, he had earlier noticed a small sign that read, TRAIL SUPPLIES. Two hours later he was up on a three-year-old gelding, sitting in a better saddle than any he had ever seen in Australia, and had a bedroll tied behind it with saddlebags stuffed full of dried food and coffee. A thick wool coat was also tied behind the saddle.

• • •

Chaddy was soon settled into a comfortable rhythm with the horse. Sitting long hours in a saddle was not a new experience for him. Prior to going after crocodiles with Moss O'Rourke, the two childhood friends worked together on Boogunda Station. It was a sheep ranch west of what would eventually become Brisbane Australia. The ranch was one of the largest in Australia, covering over quarter million acres; requiring men like Chaddy to be in the saddle for long periods as they patrolled the herds.

Boogunda was where they met Trug. His real name was Danny Truganini, an Abo; or more properly, an Australian Aboriginal. Both men had shortened their own first names from Chaderick to Chaddy, and Mossibleau (given to him by his French mother) to Moss, so it was natural that they would also chop off a portion of Danny's name. As Chaddy rocked slowly back and forth in the saddle, on the way toward the area on his map where Sutter's Mill was located, he began thinking about home. That day many years earlier, when they came across Trug, came vividly forth from his memory.

Chaddy was moving a few stray cows through the scrub brush when he heard Moss blowing on the small steel whistle that hung around each man's neck. It was their means of communicating across long distances…three short bursts followed by one long, indicated a problem. "Hold 'em boys," was all Chaddy had to say to his dogs before galloping toward Moss. He knew that the sheep would be exactly where he left them when he returned.

"What's up, mate?" He reigned up next to his friend, and accepted the small telescope Moss held out, as he nodded toward a group gathered in the distance. As Chaddy adjusted the glass to his eyes, Moss rolled a cigarette and silently waited. He treated his words the same as he did his tobacco, beer, and money—he didn't waste any. Chaddy lowered the glass. "Looks t'me like the Abos are learnin' tricks from the bloody English, and are gonna hang that black bugger."

"Yep!" Moss replaced his tobacco and retrieved a match from his small kangaroo-leather pouch. After lighting the smoke, he asked, "Whadayawannado, mate?"

Chaddy raised the glass again. After a moment, he handed it back to his friend then gave his mount a nudge with the heels of his rawhide boots. "Let's 'av a look, cobber." His horse started down from the knoll, with Moss following close behind. Minutes later the two men arrived among a group of a dozen naked aboriginal men. A young Abo, as black as any either man had ever seen, stood in the center of the group; twisting and ducking to prevent the others from putting the rope over his head. He was bloody from many abrasions where the others had beaten him with sticks and heavy branches of brush. Moss could speak many Abo dialects so when he yelled loudly **"STOP"** in the most common of the area, they all obeyed. The aboriginals knew that trouble for them would follow if they ignored the commands of a white man. In the same language he asked, "Any of you black buggers speak English?"

"Me! I do." It was the unfortunate fellow that the others had been trying to get a rope on. He was now grinning widely, sensing no doubt, possibly rescue from being the star of an 'air dance' as the English soldiers referred to a hanging. "I was a houseboy on Tasmania for the bloody Queen's own cousin, mates."

Chaddy chuckled at the memory as he plodded along toward Sutter's Mill.

Moss turned a stern eye down toward the men when he spoke again in their language. "'E works for us now boys so don't be 'angin' our bloody 'elp." He motioned to the blood covered black boy, "Get up behind my mate n' let's get the 'ell outa 'ere fore these bloodthirsty

Rick Magers

buggers decide to 'ang us all." Without hesitation the boy was astride Chaddy's horse in one nimble leap, and holding on, with his hands not quite around the massive chest of the smaller of his two rescuers.

When the two men arrived back where their dogs were keeping the sheep herd together, Chaddy finally spoke. "Let's 'av some bloody tea n' 'ere what this black little bugger 'as t'say 'bout all this." The men hopped down and hobbled their horses, surprised to see the black youth running off. They watched in amazement when he began gathering dry brush and sticks for a fire. He returned grinning, "I 'ope you blokes 'ave a bloody match, 'cause I never lived in the bush n' wouldn't 'av a clue 'ow t'start a bloody fire without one."

Chaddy struck a match and had the fire going in minutes. Moss returned with a tin pot with no handle but had a swinging wire to carry it with. It was full of water from the bag they carried, and covered with a tight fitting lid. He sat it at the edge of the fire then opened the packet he carried in the other hand. He spread a cloth on a flat rock and began carefully taking fingers full of the tealeaves from the packet and placing them on the cloth. Satisfied that he had the correct amount, he lifted the lid with his long knife's blade and set it aside so he could pour the leaves into the water. After replacing the lid he turned to the aboriginal, "Me billy only 'olds enough for the two of us, but I reckon we can do with a wee bit less so you can 'ave a sip."

"Thank you mate, thank you very much. 'Aven't 'ad m'tea since I came to visit those bloodthirsty savages."

"You came to visit them?" Chaddy looked up from the smoke he was rolling.

"Yeah mate," the boy grinned, "'at fella with the big belly an' the 'ose 'angin' down between 'is legs like a bleedin' 'orse, is me uncle."

"Damn, 'e seemed t'be the one tryin' hardest t'getcher neck in the bloody noose."

"'E was by Jesus, an 'e woulda 'ung me bloody arse if you 'adn't come t'elp me, mates." He grinned and turned from Moss to Chaddy, "Bloody well woulda, 'e would, by cracky."

The three sat silently watching the tin billy as the water came to a boil. Moss quickly grabbed the bandana from his pocket and lifted the pot from the fire. Chaddy had brought three tin cups from the tucker-bag strapped to his saddle, and set them at Moss's feet. After carefully filling all three to near equal depth he sat the billy aside. "'Elp yerself mate," he said and smiled slightly when the black boy took the smaller of the three. They all remained silent as they sipped their tea. Finally Chaddy spoke. "Alright mate, let's 'ave it. What caused those buggers to wanna 'ang you?"

The boy looked up over the top of his tin cup, "Bloody savages mates, every one o' those bush buggers are savages. Mama told me where I could find her brother and his people, so I sneaked on a freighter in Sydney and sailed away. The day after I found 'em, one of the young boys got sick. 'E was pukin' 'is guts up an' moanin' som'n awful. Next bloody day a buncha those boys started doin' the same thing. Wasn't long till one of 'em pointed at me n' said 'e's the one what brought this to us. Yeah, 'e's the one, the others started sayin' an fore long they's all pointin' at me sayin', 'bloody devil 'e is'." He finished his tea, and asked Moss if he could please borrow enough tobacco to roll himself a cigarette.

"Borrow? Y'mean t'say you'll be payin' me back, eh?"

"Bloody oath mate. I'm no slacker n' there's plenty of things I know 'ow t'do."

"Such as?" Chaddy piped in with a grin.

"Best bloody bush cook what ever put a roo in a pot mate."

"Hmmm!" Moss turned toward the boy. "Gravy? Y'make a good gravy t'simmer the bloody roo in?"

"Best bloody gravy the Queen's cousin ever 'ad in 'is mouth mates, an that's the very words 'e said." The black boy grinned wide. "'e wears today the very same bloody shoes I made 'im a year ago from the 'ide of a soft young wallaby's arse, an' I didn't need a rifle to get 'im."

"Whaja git 'im with?" Chaddy was grinning now too.

"Sling n' stone, mate."

"Well then," Chaddy said, "we'll just 'afta carry yer skinny black arse along n' see if y'can back up all this bragin' y'been blowin' about."

Moss accepted the returned tobacco pouch. He held the match as the young Abo puffed on the cigarette that he had just rolled like an old outback ranch hand. Moss then lit the one he'd just rolled for himself, and tossed the match in the fire. "One thing I'm curious about uh, uh what the bloody 'ell're we s'pose t'call you anyway?"

"Daniel Truganini, 'at's me name, an' a famous one it is mates, on Tasmania it is anyway. Most folks call me Danny."

"Trukawhat?" Chaddy asked, grinning wide.

Rick Magers

"Truganini," the boy repeated.

Before Chaddy could speak again Moss said, "Trug's as bloody far's we'll go mate. Yer Trug, long's you stick with us." Moss pulled deeply on the smoke before continuing with his original question. "Why'n bloody 'ell y'reckon they figured you t'be bringin' 'at sickness, whatever it was, to 'em?"

"'At's 'cause me mum's a spirit woman what can cast spells n' such on people. Uncle kept sayin' things like, Millie sent this evil boy to carry a spell and place it on me. We gotta 'ang the little bugger or we'll all die. Well mate, 'at was all it took. 'Em bloody savages chased me for an hour an' only caught me a wee bit before you fellas showed up." He shook his head, "Bloody good timing it was mates, or I'd be taller'n either o' you two blokes by now." His grin was becoming infectious, and even usually somber Moss was grinning more than Chaddy had ever seen his friend grin.

• • •

Chaddy reached a level spot and turned toward the low mountain peaks he had memorized from the map. He searched for the point that he was supposed to head for after climbing the hill, which his horse had just struggled up. The moment he went past a huge boulder, his horse reared up and hoofed the air ahead. A large grizzly bear was standing on its hind legs snarling at them both. Only Chaddy's years in a saddle saved them both. He waited the split second for the horse to come back down, then pulled the reins hard to the left and spun the horse around as he released the tension on the reins and prodded the horse with his heels. The horse knew exactly what the snarling beast was, and wasted no time putting distance between them and the bear. When Chaddy was a good distance away, he stopped his horse then looked back and saw the bear moving along the ridge, with two small cubs walking beside her. He shoved his floppy hat to the back of his head and wiped his brow. "What in bloody 'ell was that?" He spoke quietly aloud.

"Grizzly bear."

Chaddy spun around in his saddle, pulling the long knife from its sheath as he did.

"Easy there fella." The voice came from the thick trees beside him. "I topped this ridge just as you rounded that boulder and 'bout bumped into that ole gal."

Chaddy returned the knife and looked back and forth, searching for the man, who finally stepped out smiling. "You mighta been that grizzly's lunch if you wasn't so good in the saddle on a savvy horse." He stepped forward with his hand out, "Emerson Culpepper, Pepper to m'friends."

Chaddy leaned down to shake the small man's hand, "Chaddy O'Shea. You live around here, mate?"

"Ha!" The man laughed, "Nothing but grizzlies n' injuns live in this part of these mountains.

"What're injuns?" Chaddy looked down at the man who was dressed in animal skins and wearing shoes similar to his, but reaching almost to his knees and wrapped with rawhide strings.

"You're from the same place another fella that came through here said he was from, aincha?"

"Australia. He was probably my cobber who came 'er a bit earlier n' who I'm searchin' for. Seen 'im lately, 'ave you?"

"Not since he headed off toward Sutter's place, uh, mmm," he paused as he thought, "musta been 'bout six months ago, I reckon."

Chaddy's mouth twisted a bit as he shook his head slowly. "What're injuns?" He repeated.

The mountain man turned and motioned with his arm, and a moment later a thin Miwok Indian emerged from behind a tree. He walked slowly forward, his eyes never leaving Chaddy. He listened as the man in skins spoke; his black eyes still locked on Chaddy. He shook his head slightly then relaxed his stance, resting on the long muzzleloader, but still watching the stranger on the horse. "Here's one you can look at yerself. He's a Meewuk from a tribe down aways," he pointed toward the area north of San Francisco. "I hired him a coupla years ago to help me trap beaver, so I can keep searchin' for the gold I know's in these mountains right 'round here som'rs."

"G'day mate," Chaddy nodded toward the Indian who nodded back. "Are there more of 'em or are 'im n' 'is folks all there is?"

"Boy oh boy," the crusty old mountain man leaned on his own muzzleloader, "you sure don't know much about this place do ya?"

"Wasn't even sure which bloody way the boat was goin', and the pommy captain 'ad never been 'ere either, so wasn't any way for me

Rick Magers

t'learn." Chaddy looked around then continued, "Ain't a bit like Australia. Only thing that might bitecha, 'cept the snakes, n' we 'ave plenty o' those buggers, would be a crazy dingo. Then all ya gotta do is kick 'im in 'is arse n' off he goes." He grinned and noticed that the Indian relaxed a bit. "An Abo eats the bloody things when they start gettin' feisty, n' swear they taste better'n roo meat. A roo'll kick yer bloody 'ead off if ya mess with 'im, but 'e'll leave ya alone if y'don't bother 'im." He nodded toward where the bear encounter happened, "I reckon 'at beast'd eat me 'orse too, after 'e 'ad me for 'is lunch."

"They ain't t'be messed with, that's for sure. What the heck's a dingo, a roo and an Abo?"

Chaddy grinned mischievously, "Y'don't know much atol about Australia, do ya? An Abo's a black savage that wanders about, livin' off the land, a roo's a kangaroo, and a dingo's a dog." He pulled the makings of a cigarette from the pocket of the heavy coat he'd put on earlier, and began rolling one. As he was returning the pouch to his pocket, he nodded toward the Indian, "Is 'at bloke a bloody savage?"

The man smiled, then turned and spoke to the Indian who grinned wide, nodding his head up and down. Chaddy grinned, "Better'n our bloody Abo; naked bastards think they're people."

"They dangerous?"

"Ha! Too bloody lazy, those buggers."

"How long're you plannin' t'stay here?"

"Long's it takes t'find me fair dinkum cobber, or learn what 'appened to 'im."

"Well, as I recall he was heading to old man Sutter's place from here, but dunno what his plans were from there."

Chaddy looked back again where the grizzly had been, "'At fella Sutter sell supplies?"

"Yeah, he keeps some stuff around t'sell, but gets an arm n' a leg for everything. Why? Whacha need?"

"A pair o' long leg pants, n' after seeing that beast," he nodded toward the bear incident, "I reckon I oughta get m'self a rifle."

"Getcherself some good running shoes too, fella 'cause you'll need 'em if you shoot one o' those grizzlies."

A quizzical expression crossed Chaddy's face, "Why's 'at mate?"

"Cause all you do when you shoot one o' those mean son of a bitches is piss 'em off, n' if you do that, you better drop yer gun n' run hard's y'can."

Rick Magers

Chaddy shoved his hat back a bit farther and scratched his head, "Wild country y'got 'ere mate." He took a drag from his cigarette then asked, "Any other beasts around like 'im what'll drag yer arse 'ome for tucker or eat you right where 'e bloody jumped ya?"

The mountain man turned to the Indian again and spoke in his language. The Miwok grinned as he waved his free hand and arm from as far left as he could reach, then swept it to the far right, and said something to his companion, who turned back to Chaddy. "He said there are many things out there that will eat us, and we also will eat them, but they are usually much better equipped to do it."

"Bloody Jesus, bigger'n that beast?"

"The jaguars and cougars aren't as big, but they're smart and wait quietly till you're close enough for 'em to jump you. There's one though, a good ways north o' here that's as big as a grizzly and twice as mean."

"Bloody oath mate, what's 'at?"

"Bull Moose. Meanest thing on four legs, and that grizzly woulda turned and got the hell outa his way if it'd been him instead of you comin' around that boulder."

"They around here, mate?"

"Nope and be damned glad of it too. They're farther north, but that don't mean some of 'em mightn't come wanderin' down this way, so if you see one don't mess with him."

"What's 'e look like anyway, the bloody devil 'is ownself?"

"The devil couldn't be that ugly, fella. This thing stands taller'n yer horse and has a spread of horns big enough to lift that horse and toss him over his rear end," the old man grinned and added, "with you still in the saddle."

Chaddy shook his head slowly, "By Jesus mate, I'm thinkin' y'll never tame this wild land."

"I hope not, 'cause I like it just the way it is." The mountain man turned to his Indian friend and spoke in his language. Chaddy grinned when the Modoc grunted and nodded that he agreed with his friend.

"Yeah! I reckon I feel the same about Australia. I 'ope it never gets so civilized that ships start bringin' loads o' folks t'live there." He turned and looked in the direction he was headed and asked, "'Ow many days y'reckon it'll take me t'get to that Sutter blokes place?"

"Two, maybe three days. Won't be no hard weather 'roun that area for awhile, so you shouldn't have any problems gettin' there."

Rick Magers

"Well mate," Chaddy said as he adjusted himself in the saddle, "best I be gettin' on m'way then, and thanks for the information."

"Yeah, we've gotta get to the river n' check our traps. Keep yer eyes peeled for grizzlies fella, 'cause there's plenty of 'em 'roun here." He nodded his head and walked off toward the woods near the area that Chaddy had met the bear. The slender Modoc nodded slightly and followed the mountain man.

The following day, Chaddy was up long before dawn and moving toward Sutter's Mill. Either because of something different about the way his horse was behaving or simple intuition, Chaddy was tense. He had shifted his big knife and sheath around to the front so it could be easily reached. Even though the mornings were cold, he hadn't tied his jacket's rawhide strings together. The handle of the knife awaited, a couple of inches from his right hand as his left held the reins. His eyes scanned left and right, as his head remained motionless. His ears were straining to hear any unusual sound. As suddenly as a startled grouse flies, Chaddy's eyes and ears were both sending signals to his brain. His hand was immediately clutching the knife's handle as his eyes caught sight of the Indians stepping onto the path ahead. His ears had already heard the lone Indian who was attempting to surprise his prey from behind, before the white man knew he was there. The youthful Indian brave could not possibly have known that his prey was very used to listening for the stealthy Australian Dingo to slip in amongst the sheep for an easy kill.

The young Indian rushed forward on what he thought were silent moccasins, only to feel the sharp edge of the white man's huge knife, entering his skull just above his nose...it was his final ambush. Chaddy brought the bloody blade forward and down to his side as he urged the horse to leap fast ahead, while leaning low and hugging his mount's neck.

Startled by their friend's failed ambush, the three young bucks' timing was thrown off. Before they could regain the lost advantage they initially had, Chaddy's sharp knife blade had sliced across the neck of one, and moments later entered the chest of another—point first. When he saw the remaining Indian running into the woods, Chaddy lay lower still and urged the horse ahead at a fast gallop. He had no way of knowing that there were only four Indians, and he wasn't the type to wait around to find out.

Rick Magers

A short run up the hill for his horse brought Chaddy to a treeless area where he could survey the terrain that he'd just crossed. With eyes accustomed to spotting anything unusual moving amongst his sheep, he searched every nook and cranny below. His picketed horse grazed on lush, high-mountain grass as Chaddy lay atop a large boulder searching for movement. Two hours later he was satisfied that the savages who had attempted to ambush him had not followed. Back aboard his mount, he continued toward Sutter's Mill.

• • •

The swelling in Frenchy's hand began going down after one full day of soaking in the solution of medicinal salts given to him by the only doctor in the Yerba Buena area. Doc Sven Munssen wasn't really a medical doctor. He'd learned a bit of veterinary medicine along the way, and drank whiskey with a dentist in a Five Points brothel, a tough section of New York City. Sven learned fast by simply listening to the procedures his dentist friend described, but a fifth ace discovered in his sleeve during a poker game, hastened his departure from New York.

He now held Frenchy's hand after a good long soaking, "Nothin' busted Frenchy, or that swelling wouldn't have gone down this fast."

Frenchy looked at his hand as he moved all four fingers and wiggled his thumb. "Yeah doc, don't reckon there is." He looked up grinning, "Time I ketch up with that feriner, this hand'll be ready to choke him till he messes his britches." The grin widened, "Or whatever the hell them short little kiddie pants're called." When Doc Sven reached to begin bandaging the hand again, Frenchy pulled it away and stood. "I got som'n to take care of and that dern bandage might get in m'way."

He turned after opening the door to Doc's office & sleeping quarters, "I'll pay ya when I gits my money from Jim Fenster." He turned, ducked to miss hitting his head against the top of the doorway, and walked out."

Cheap bastard, Doc Sven thought as he cleaned up the mess, *he'll pay me like he has for all the other times I've fixed him up after gettin' shot or stabbed.* He went to the door and tossed out the basin of water that Frenchy had been soaking his hand in. Back at the table, he poured himself a large glass of whiskey and sat down thinking. *Next time he gets wounded, I'll put some rotten meat inside the wound and sew him up. That'll be the end of that no good stingy Frog.*

Darkness that same night found Frenchy waiting near the cabin that Homer, Joshua, and Elmo shared. An hour of patient waiting yielded the exact results he was counting on. The three old men came around the corner of the huge building, and proceeded unsteadily toward their cabin on drunken legs. Frenchy moved silently in the darkness until he was close to the men. Homer worked noisily as he attempted to get the skeleton key into the latch on the door. Frenchy moved close as they all three entered, and waited for the lamp to be lit. He knew that the two would be standing just inside, waiting for the light. The moment it came on, Frenchy stepped inside and closed the door. With his foot holding the door shut, preventing any escape, he pulled one of his pistols from the wide belt and pointed it at Elmo's chest. The explosion startled the other two, but they simply couldn't move. Like a deer facing a bright light shined into its eyes, they stood with their mouths open as Frenchy replaced that pistol and pulled another from his belt. The second blast almost took Joshua's head off because the barrel of the flintlock was but a few inches from the man's neck.

Before Homer could move, Frenchy had his skinny neck gripped in his good right hand—the same one that had just sent Homer's two pals to the promised land. "Whaja tell that funny talkin' guy you was a'drawin' that map fer?"

Too much whiskey combined with two blasts from the pistols had rendered Homer totally incapable of replying. His pale tongue was protruding far out, and his eyes were bugging from their sockets. Frenchy threw the old man back against the log wall, then drew the huge knife from the same belt that now held the two empty pistols. He grabbed the old man with his left hand and winced at the pain. "You're the old son-of-a-bitch that caused me to get this smashed hand." He withdrew his left hand and with the right shoved the knife into Homer's belly. Still the old man was speechless, and stood like a robot as Frenchy slit his throat.

The huge man easily tossed the three men beneath the old wood table then picked up a chair and with one mighty swing shattered it and the table. He threw wooden articles onto the pile then poured the contents of the can of lamp oil sitting near the door, all over everything. He gripped the glowing lamp in his sore left hand, and prepared to open the door. The moment that the lamp hit the pile of wood and dead bodies, Frenchy was out the door and moving stealthily, but swiftly, away from the cabin. Far at the other end of the area behind the buildings that made up the town of Yerba Buena, he watched as the small cabin roared into flames, many reaching high into the nearby trees.

Damn! Frenchy was disappointed, because he loved to start and watch fires. *I thought sure then dern flames'd get into them buildings n' burn the whole town down.*

He watched as the townspeople carried buckets of stored seawater, but couldn't stop the fire. They began splashing water on the closest building and let the small cabin burn to ashes. The three old men weren't missed for almost two days. By that time there was little left, and Frenchy was following Chaddy's trail into the mountains. *I heard them old guys a'talkin' in the bar enough to know about where that guy went.* His black eyes searched the trail ahead as his horse climbed higher and higher into the mountains. *He's headin' right where that other guy what talked funny like him went.*

● ● ●

Chaddy's horse climbed the narrow winding trail up the mountain, finally stepping out onto a flattened area that had obviously been cleared of many trees. Far at the other end, he spotted what appeared to be a pile of material and a building of some sort being constructed. When he had cut the distance in half, he saw a stout man with large sideburns and a bushy mustache, sitting on the stump of a tree. Beyond him were several bearded men sitting about on stumps and boulders, as women in bulky dresses and bonnets carried plates of food to them.

"G'day mates," Chaddy yelled as he waved his floppy leather hat, "do y'mind if I join you?"

The stout man stood and motioned for him to proceed. When Chaddy was near enough to hear, the old man said, "I'm Captain John Sutter, who might you be, sir?"

Chaddy eased gracefully from his horse and extended his hand, "Chaddy O'Shea sir, and I'm right happy to see someone other than bloody savages."

After shaking hands, Captain Sutter asked, "run into some Indians, did you?"

"Yeah, back down a good piece, but I reckon they musta decided to carry their dead 'ome rather than follow me, 'cause I've not seen 'em since."

The other men remained silent, and Capt. Sutter just stared at the man standing in short pants like the young boys in Yerba Buena wear in summertime. Finally he spoke, "Killed one of the Indians, didja?"

"Three I reckon mate, unless they're a 'elluva lot tougher than our Abo's." Chaddy spoke in a matter-of-fact tone with no braggadocio in his voice, as he looked around.

"What are Abo's?"

"Savages! Just like those buggers, but blacker'n a sinners 'eart. What're those savages called?"

"What kinda clothes were they wearing?" After listening to Chaddy's description of the Indians he'd encountered, Capt. Sutter answered his question. "Sounds like a group of Miwok that broke away from their main camp to start raising hell. Young buncha bucks just causin' trouble for their own people and everyone else. Came through here a month ago and we had t'kill a few of 'em." He nodded with his head toward the men, who were ignoring the two men talking, as they continued eating their lunch. "I found out just how tough those Mormons can be when they're pushed."

"What country are those blokes from?"

"Ain't never heard o' Mormons?"

"Nope, not that I recall."

"They're a religion, but they come from all over." He nodded toward the group eating, "One o' them came to this country from Germany a few years ago."

"Hmmm!" Chaddy observed them a moment before turning back to John Sutter. "How come those bloody savages are tryin' t'kill people like me what's just movin' along n' mindin' me own damn business?"

"Too darn many folks movin' in to look for gold, and it's pushing the Indians off their own land. A few small groups of mostly young bucks are jumpin' the miners when they can, and waylaying white travelers wherever they find 'em. Many miners will shoot them Indians quicker'n they'll shoot a snake."

"That much gold 'ere about, huh?"

"Not really, or at least no big strikes that I've heard about. I just reckon that white folks and Indians're never gonna get along." He turned to face Chaddy as he asked with a nod toward him, "Gold what you're up here lookin' for?"

"Nossir, but I was told that my fair dinkum cobber came this way, lookin' for the stuff."

"Your what?"

"Fair dinkum cobber." He stared a moment at Captain Sutter, "me mate…you know, best friend."

"You're from that island out yonder aincha?" He nodded toward the west with his chin. "Another fella, your friend probably, came through here a few months ago, and he was from there too. Australia it's called, ain't it?"

"Right you are mate, and a lovely place too, without creatures like a bloody bear, bigger'n the two of us, jumpin' out to eatcha."

"Met a grizzly, didja?"

"Yeah mate, and it's thrilled I'll be t'never meet another."

"Reckon I feel the same about those beasts."

"'Ow long did my mate stay around 'ere?"

"Not long atol. He bought a few things he thought he'd need, then headed north. He was with a couple o' fellas from up in Canada. They all three came back through here a coupla months later, then we never saw 'em again."

"Yeah, that was 'im, 'cause some old gents told me that 'e was teamed with two Canadian blokes." Chaddy looked north in the direction that his friend and companions had gone, "Wild bloody land up that way mate, so I reckon my cobber's gonna be 'ard to track."

"Sure is," Captain Sutter replied, "men go up into those Rocky Mountains and ain't ever heard from again."

"'E's a tough lad though cap'n, so I reckon 'e'll be looking out for 'is own arse n' 'is mates too."

"You plan to follow his track on up into those mountains?"

"Yep! 'E's me fair dinkum cobber, so I'll keep lookin' till I find 'im," he paused a moment then added, "or what's left of 'im." He looked about then asked, "Is there a place where I can hobble m'horse and spread out a blanket t'sleep on tonight?" He grinned at the old man, "One where them bloody grizzies won't be sneakin' in t'eat me n' me 'orse durin' the night."

"Before we began building the big house where the mill will be, we built us a small bunk house and storage building." He pointed to a spot beneath a stand of tall trees, a short distance from the Mormon men, now moving around in preparation to return to work. "That one," he joggled his finger at the smaller of the two, sitting a good distance from the other log building, "is the bunk house, and the other one's the storage shed." He turned back to Chaddy, "Your welcome to bunk in with us if you like."

"Thank you sir, but no. Australia's a big, wide open land with few roofs and I've been beneath few of 'em…don't plan t'be under more'n I must." He pointed to a spot of grass near the trees that he'd noticed when he entered Capt. Sutter's compound. "'Ow y'reckon that'd be for a night spot?"

"Fine's any other around here, and you won't have to worry about the Miwok, 'cause we been keeping a watch at night since them braves started all this crap." He turned back to Chaddy; "Grizzlies won't come around a camp with men unless there's food left layin' around. We put up every speck, and have a hole in the ground inside the bunkhouse where we keep the rest in a box with a cover on it."

"That'll be fine sir, and do y'think I could pay for my tucker and eat with you folks tonight?" He nodded toward the area the men had been sitting, "I saw the plates o' tucker the women were handin' the men and m'stomach started tryin' to eat me belt."

"Sure can, and I ain't et the noon meal m'self, so hobble your horse on that grass n' we'll have us a bite before them ladies put it all away for later."

After the two men finished their lunch, Chaddy asked about supplies. "Well," the captain said as he wiped his tin plate clean with a biscuit, "I've been building up supplies by packing them up here on every group heading this way. Jim Fenster has a list and he puts whatever he can on the groups comin' up; miners and wannabe gold digging millionaires, I reckon?" He stood after handing one of the Mormon ladies his plate, "C'mon and we'll have a look n' see what you might be needin'.." After one step he stopped and looked at Chaddy, "What kinda buyin' money y'got?"

"Gold nuggets." Chaddy pulled a small leather pouch from the saddlebags he'd thrown over his shoulder, after securing his horse in the middle of the grass. "No big'ns mind you, but good quality gold." He handed one to the captain.

"Yes, by Jove, very high quality indeed, compared to what I've seen." He handed it back, "Get it in your country?"

Rick Magers

"Yeah," he tied the saddlebag shut again, "we didn't find a lot of it, but what we found was all like those."

"This fella that you're searching for was with you?"

"Yeah," we've been good mates since we were children, but Moss heard some sailors talking about all the gold being found in the new country across the water. I figured it was silly crossing an ocean to find gold when we were finding it right where we were tendin' our bloody sheep." He shook his head slowly, "next thing I knew, ole Moss was on a bloody English ship and sailin' away."

"If you've got a bunch of them nuggets in those saddlebags son, don't let nobody find out, 'cause folks do strange things when that darn stuff comes out."

"Not on yer life mate, would I carry a buncha those nuggets into the bush. Nah! I buried a pouch near Yerba Buena the night before I 'eaded up 'ere, then buried another back down the trail aways."

Capt. Sutter shook his head up and down slowly, "Good thinking lad, good thinking indeed."

The following dawn found Chaddy a couple of miles along the trail that wound its way through the forest. He was dressed in a long sleeve, heavy wool shirt—full-length pants, held up by a wide leather belt. A significant addition to his wardrobe was the small pistol shoved behind the belt. It was invented only a short time earlier in Belgium. Capt. Sutter had traded gold searching tools for the Mariette Pepperbox. The entire six shot pistol was only a bit over seven inches long. Properly cared for and loaded according to the manufacturer's instructions, a copy of which came with the weapon, it was reliable. With a 9mm ball roaring out from the slightly less than three-inch-long barrel, at 500 feet a second, it was lethal in the hands of a man who would practice with it...Chaddy was that kind of man. His destination was a gold mining camp below the ridge he was following by the light of a full moon, pre-dawn morning.

He stopped at noon to hobble his horse so it could graze a while, as Chaddy paced off a few feet's distance from a small sapling. For an hour he repeatedly fired the six barrels, one at a time, at the sapling, then reloaded and began again. When the sapling was so weakened from being hit by the lead balls, and began weeping toward the ground, Chaddy re-loaded the Mariette, returned the pouch of powder and reloading supplies to his saddlebags, re-mounted the horse he'd named Spooky, and continued toward the mining camp.

Rick Magers

Even though the captain, and the Mormons who were helping him build the mill, soon to become world famous as the site of the largest gold strike ever, seemed like good folks, he slept little...always cautious—ever watchful. He decided he would find a secure spot to stop and get a good night's rest, even if he didn't sleep much, then continue on to the camp in the morning. He had noticed how the horse was calm when nothing or no one was nearby, but would become very jumpy when a strange animal of any kind was close enough for him to smell—even man...especially man. Chaddy thought Spooky a good name and relied on the horse to alert him. An hour before dark, he located a good secure place to spend the night.

Moving steadily closer to Sutter's Mill, Frenchy slouched in the saddle dozing, as the huge horse climbed higher and higher into the Rocky Mountains. Periodically the huge bearded man opened his eyes to take a pull on the bladder full of wine, scan the terrain ahead, and then returned to his dozing.

Chaddy entered the gold camp and slowly walked Spooky along the path between the rows of makeshift quarters, which the miners had erected. Most of the miners were at their nearby diggings, so only a few people remained in camp. One young boy about twelve came running when he spotted Chaddy. "Howdy mister, come lookin' fer gold, didja?"

Chaddy smiled down at the youth, "No lad, didn't come lookin' fer a bloody thing except me fair dinkum cobber."

"You talk funny mister, just like that other guy what found this place did."

Chaddy's mind was reeling from hearing that his friend was actually in the very same camp that he'd just ridden into, but noticing that a woman was paying obvious attention to the boy's chatter, he remained impassive as he commented, "still around 'ere is 'e?"

"Oh nossir, he and his pals took off right after we came here." The boy jumped slightly when the woman yelled for him to get on with his business...he took off running.

"G'day ma'am, a nice lad 'e is I reckon. Yours, is 'e?"

"Yes," she scowled, "an it's easy t'see that he's not right in the head, running right up to a stranger like he did."

"Well," Chaddy smiled broadly, "M'name's Chaddy O'Shea, so

we're not strangers now."

She ignored him and returned to the huge pile of clothing that she was scrubbing in a big round wooden tub. Chaddy paused a few moments, then nudged his horse with the heels of his new boots; used but new to him. The trail had tents and wooden lean-to shelters scattered along it. In the center sat a small closed-in wooden wagon with a padlocked door. Another smaller, open, hauling wagon was sitting nearby. A large canvas and an assortment of slender poles created an awning in front. Several chair-height severed tree stumps had been dragged beneath the awning, sat upright, and had names carved on each. A grizzled old man wearing a stovepipe hat sat in a hand made chair behind a split-log bar. On it sat a bottle of whiskey, and several small, thick glasses.

Chaddy dismounted and tied Spooky to the long lodgepole pine sitting between two forked sticks buried in the ground. "Y'wouldn't 'ave beer I reckon, wouldja mate?"

"Nope, but plenty o' damn good whiskey." The man remained motionless with his arms crossed and his hands beneath his armpits, but Chaddy noticed that his eyes did a thorough search of him and his horse. "Wanna sell 'at 'ere horse? I know a fella what'll pay you good for it, and all in genuine gold nuggets." Still no smile or movement, except his lips.

Chaddy stooped beneath the low front of the makeshift awning and entered. "An just 'ow in the bloody 'ell then would I be gettin' outa these mountains?" Before the man could answer, Chaddy pointed at the bottle of whiskey, "Let's 'av a bit o' that, mate."

The man leaned far forward and poured a glass full then returned the cork to the bottle and watched Chaddy.

"I'll be damned if that ain't bloody good whiskey, mate." He shoved the glass to the edge so the old man could refill it. Before lifting the glass, he asked, "Been 'ere a long while, 'ave you?"

"I came up with Frenchy when he first set this place up for old man Fenster, n' ain't been off this here rock since." He poured Chaddy and himself a glass of whiskey then returned to his previous posture, balancing the glass on his leg. "You come up lookin' for gold?"

Chaddy sipped a bit before answering, "Lookin' for my mate. 'E came 'ere a while back n' I ain't 'eard a word in a while." He sipped again as he looked straight into the old man's eyes. "I reckon 'e was 'ere a while back." Another sip, "Whadaya reckon mate? Was 'at 'im what came through 'ere with a coupla Canadians?" One more small sip, "Talks like me 'e does and is a big bloke, n' 'as a full head o' red hair." He stood with the glass and stared into the man's eyes, until the old bartender lifted the glass to sip as he tried to match Chaddy's intense, unblinking stare. He failed, and shifted his gaze as he tossed the whiskey down.

"Yeah," he finally answered, "he musta been one of the guys that Frenchy made a deal with to take over this claim."

The name Frenchy rang a bell in Chaddy's head. "Frenchy huh? 'E that dark fella that works for Fenster and Bullock?"

"Ain't no Bullock now." The old man poured another glass of whiskey, but spoke before tossing it down, "Brady Bullock died right after he n' Jim Fenster got that place in Yerba Buena up n' runnin' good." Chaddy remained silent as the man drank the shot. "Fell down the darn stairs and broke his neck." He motioned with the bottle, "Ready for another one?"

Chaddy lifted his half full glass. "No mate, I'll just sip a bit, 'cause I'm 'eadin' on to a place called," he removed a scrap of paper from his new shirt's pocked and read, "Mugfuzzle Flat. Sounds t'me like the kinda place ole' Moss would 'ead toward." He sipped a little then said, "Whadayathink, mate?"

"Yes by golly, come t'think of it, that's where I think they said they was a'headin' when they left here."

Chaddy tossed down the rest of the whiskey and sat the glass down. "Well mate, in that case I best get on me way. 'Ow much I owe ya for the liquor?"

"Three shots is a pea nugget if you're carryin' gold, which's about the onliest thing we trade with up here."

Chaddy removed his nugget pouch and removed a small gold nugget. "I reckon me two shots then oughta be a nugget like this, what's a wee bit smaller'n a pea, eh mate?" He replaced the pouch then tossed the nugget on the table, and hooked his left thumb in the leather belt as his right arm remained near the huge knife. The old man had been looking at the odd little pistol's handle protruding from Chaddy's belt, and hadn't noticed the knife.

"Two was it? Well then you're right, that's the exact size nugget for two shots."

The first thing Chaddy noticed when he entered was a long barreled rifle, leaning within arm's reach of the old man in the stovepipe hat. He moved casually sideways until he was at the edge of the awning. "I'll be gettin' on me way then mate, and I'll stop back by for s'more o' that good whiskey." Keeping an eye on the man and the musket, he untied Spooky and mounted. He then urged the horse backwards, all the while keeping his eyes on the man. *Som'n about that old bugger makes me think 'e'd shoot a man for 'is bloody shoes.* Still watching the man, he nudged Spooky and headed out of the camp.

"It's that dark fella from down in Yerba Buena." Capt. Sutter handed the long telescope to the young Mormon. "Take a good look and see if you can spot anybody else with him. I don't trust that one; he's got an evil look in his eyes." He turned when he heard a noise, and saw that three of the older Mormons were walking toward him with muskets in their hands. They positioned themselves near trees and silently waited.

"Howdy Cap'n Sutter, how's the mill comin' along?"

"Fair t'midlin' I s'pose."

"Gonna have a roof over it by winter?"

"We're 'bout ready to begin' puttin' planks up there, so I reckon we'll have 'er dry by time it starts snowin' hard."

"Good, 'cause Mister Fenster has a boat load of miners comin' from Ireland that're gonna come up here to work his claim, and they're gonna need supplies." The entire time Frenchy was talking, his eyes were roaming. "Ain't seen a funny talkin' guy wearing short kiddie pants comin' through here, didja?"

"Ain't been nary a soul this way in a coon's age." He didn't understand why he spontaneously lied, but he didn't like Frenchy, and wanted him on his way.

"Well, reckon I'll get on down to the camp now, n' see how everything's going." He pulled his horse's head around and headed out on the same trail that Chaddy had taken a couple of days earlier.

"Psssssst, hey mister."

Chaddy was a couple of miles from the camp when the same young boy he'd met when he first entered the camp, hailed him from the brush. He stopped Spooky and looked to where the voice had come from. "C'mon out lad, what's on your mind?" The boy stepped from behind a tree no farther away than a long reach. Chaddy was impressed by the boy's stealth. "Pretty good job o' stayin' outa sight lad. Me Abo mates'd be impressed."

"What's a meyabo?"

"Abo, not meyabo. They're a wee bit like the Indians you 'av 'ereabouts, but black as a moonless night, and they can walk right up behind you without you 'earin' a bloody sound. Sneaky buggers they are, by Jesus."

"Black like Frenchy?"

"If it's the Frenchy I met, then they'd make 'im look like a frightened ghost. "This Frenchy you're talkin' about live down near the water in Yerba Buena?"

"Yeah, that's the one, and he's the one what beat me with a stick and busted m'leg." He pulled his pant's leg up to reveal a crooked leg. "See how crooked it is now?"

"Like a bloody dog's 'ind leg it is alright. Why'd 'e do that?"

"He was nekkid in the tent with my ma when I come walkin' in, but I swear I didn't know they's in there."

"Well lad, what I saw of 'im makes me think 'e'd be a good'n to stay away from."

"I'm gonna shoot him if'n I can get that big ole rifle away from Bones."

"Is 'e that fella what sells the whiskey?"

"Yeah, and he's as bad as Frenchy." The boy nervously glanced around then lowered his voice, "I'll tell ya som'n if'n you'll give me that big knife y'got."

"Can't part with it lad, but if what you tell me's worth it, I 'ave a small folding knife that I'll letcha 'ave, an' it's sharp enough t'shave a beaver with."

The youth glanced nervously around again then said, "Frenchy and his friend Bones kilt that friend o' yours, so's they could have that gold diggin' camp where me n' ma live."

A moment later the boy closed the pocketknife and put in securely in the pocket of his pants before dashing into the brush and disappearing. Chaddy slowly eased Spooky from the trail then started carefully working his way through the overgrown vegetation, back toward the mining camp he'd left behind only a short time earlier. He located a good spot to leave the horse, then after hobbling it in the center of a grassy patch on the sunny side of a huge boulder, he began stealthily moving toward the mining camp. When he had the first tent in sight, he lay down beneath some heavy brush to rest till dark. He lay there thinking, *'fore I'm finished with 'im, I reckon that Bones fella in the tall hat'll tell me if it was he n' Frenchy that killed Moss n' 'is mates.*

Chaddy awoke after dark and saw fires burning along the entire length of the camp. *Gettin' the evening's tucker ready, I reckon.* He began moving toward the closed-in wagon where he had enjoyed some whiskey awhile earlier. A cautious hour later, he was within hearing distance from the old man who was still wearing his tall stovepipe hat.

Unknown to Chaddy, an old woman's eyes had been following him since he moved silently past her crude lean-to. The half Miwok Indian—half Mexican woman had inherited eagle eyesight from her ancestors, and could spot movement at night that few could—until it was too late. She heard a sound at the other end of their camp, and began moving stealthily along the ridge above the path. Moments later she beckoned the rider, "Pssst."

The rider stopped, squinting into the darkness as he withdrew a pistol from his belt. "Who's there?" He said quietly.

"Me," she whispered, "Hookeye. I have something to sell."

The rider nudged the huge horse toward the voice in the dark, which he recognized as a valuable source of information.

Chaddy lay silently nearby for an hour, as the old man chewed on something that had been cooking on a steel skewer over the fire…and sipped whiskey. *I wish to bloody 'ell I had eaten some tucker before comin' 'ere t'watch this old buzzard.* His eyes narrowed to slits when he heard the sound of a horse coming. Presently, the horse stopped at the same rail that Spooky was tied to earlier in the day. When Frenchy ducked to enter the area beneath the canvas that covered the sitting-stumps and split-log bar, light from the fire just beyond the cover illuminated his huge dark face. Chaddy was delighted to see the man, who he was now certain had slaughtered his friend.

"What's up old bandit?" Frenchy grinned at the old man in the tall stovepipe hat.

"Knowing you as long as I have," Bones answered solemnly, "probably the price of whiskey." He watched warily as the big man lumbered toward the fire with a stump in his hands. After positioning it near the end of the log bar, he grabbed the bottle that Bones shoved toward him.

Get good n' bloody drunk you fat bastard, Chaddy thought as he lay watching, *and it won't be the back edge o' me blade that you'll be feelin' this time.* He lay silent for an hour as the two men drank whiskey. When Frenchy stood, turned, and looked in the direction of where he lay, Chaddy had a strange feeling rush through him—too late. Before he could consider what had caused the feeling, two burly men pounced upon him. Before he could get his hand to his knife or pistol, he felt the blow from a heavy object, and the dark world instantly became darker.

A short time later Chaddy began regaining consciousness, but he instinctually remained motionless. He realized that his hands and feet were hog-tied behind his back, and he was lying on wooden boards, rather than the ground where he was attacked. *Sorry bloody fix I got m'self into this time,* he thought as his aching head began to clear. *Musta been that kid I gave me pocketknife to, who told 'em that I was 'ere in their camp.* Awhile later, he was still pondering his dilemma, when he felt something touching his bound hands. Instantly they were free, and an almost silent voice whispered into his ear, "They're lookin' for me, then they're gonna kill us both." Chaddy felt his legs being released from the ropes also, then the voice returning to his ear. "Here's my mom's old gun. It only has one bullet but it's a big'n, and I checked to be sure that it's ready."

Chaddy's senses were now at the peak of their alertness. He eased up and looked over the edge of the open wagon that he'd been thrown into. The fire was still burning a short distance away, and he could easily hear the two men talking. "When Brutt and Tad find that brat what was seen talkin' to that little sissypants squirt who messed up m'hand, we'll carry 'em both in the wagon to where we buried them other guys, and I'll cut their throats with that little pissant's own damn knife. Ha, ha, ha, boy-oh-boy, that's great...his own knife. Bloody knife, he'd say. Ha, ha, ha, hoboy, hoboy, bloody knife. Haw, haw, haw, I love it."

The two men, who had apparently been searching for the boy that Chaddy had given the pocketknife to, returned to the campfire. One said, "Can't find that kid anywhere."

The other added, "We'll have us a coupla glasses of whiskey t'warm our bones, then keep lookin' till we find him."

Frenchy glared at the two men but remained silent as he stood. He looked with disgust at them and headed toward the open wagon. Chaddy had already cocked the pistol during their talking, so he lay on his back waiting. When Frenchy's huge head peered over the edge, it was backlit by the campfire—just enough for Chaddy to see where to place the barrel. The explosion knocked the Frenchman back, and Chaddy was following him closely as he leapt from the wagon. Frenchy was dead before he was prone on the ground, with half of his head missing. Chaddy dropped the pistol as soon as he pulled the trigger and was now atop Frenchy, feeling for his own pistol or Frenchy's. He soon located both of Frenchy's Chatellerault single shot pistols. He had them both up, cocked, and aimed as the two men regained their wits and rushed toward him. The first blast hit one in the chest when he was still three feet distance. The second man had his long hunting knife up and was almost to Chaddy when the second lead ball tore through his flimsy shirt and on into his heart.

Chaddy dropped both empty pistols, and was back at Frenchy's body, frantically searching for his own six-shot pepperbox or his knife, when another explosion roared through the camp. He looked up to see the skinny old man, still wearing his stovepipe hat, standing above him with a double-edged axe raised to strike. Chaddy intuitively rolled away as Bones' legs gave way and he fell to the ground. Still running on pure adrenaline, Chaddy returned to his search of the Frenchman's dead body. He finally located his small pistol, shoved into Frenchy's belt, and his knife in its sheath hanging from a rope around the man's neck—or what was left of it. He cocked the pistol and drew the knife from the sheath, then looked around. The boy was standing with the bartender's long musket.

"He sure woulda shotcha," the boy grinned wide, "but I'd already grabbed it n' run into the dark."

Chaddy slowly stood and looked cautiously around. "Y'reckon there's any more of 'em?"

"Nope! Them's the same four what kilt my paw and them fellers you been lookin' for." He leaned the musket back against the closed-in wagon and smiled again. "This camp'll probably be alright now, doncha reckon?"

Chaddy moved to the split-log bar and sat upon one of the stumps. After a glass of whiskey, he poured another, then before drinking it he answered the boy. "Yeah! Reckon it will, mate."

THE END

Rick Magers

2

BUFFALO and MEN

Jesse McKannah had been with the Flathead Indians for two years. Meeting Prairie Rose gave him a reason to live, and he was as excited as the Flathead Indians to be arriving on the plateaus where they would hunt their life-partners—buffalo. It was a difficult journey but with Jesse's help they had survived attacks from their ancient enemy, the Blackfoot, and had lost none of their people.

"There is no food so pleasant to eat as buffalo tongue," the Chief said to no one in particular…just musing as he neared the top of the bluff. "I could eat it every night at the campfire for as many passings of mother sun as the Great Spirit would give me."

"And there is no meat so tender," Jesse commented, "as a chunk from the rear of the buffalo."

"Yes, and the many wonderful things the women make from the parts inside the belly." The chief spurred his horse on, and leaned forward as the beast climbed up the last rise to the top, overlooking the lake and plateau beyond.

The Chief' was stunned, "Where could they have all gone?"

Lame Wolverine left the trail to join the chief and his friend. He was also stunned to see a vast empty area…where they expected thousands of buffalo to be grazing. "Have they gone to the other side of the world?" All three men sat on their horses; a deathly silence filling the air around them.

After several minutes, Jesse broke the silence, "I think my people are responsible for this. When I got my trapping supplies, I heard stories about large caravans of white men killing buffalo by the thousands."

The Chief looked at Jesse. "Why? White men do not use buffalo. They do not eat it, make their homes from it, or sleep under it."

"They are killing your people by killing buffalo."

"Why do the white men want to kill my people? We have always treated the white men with honor, and made them welcome guests in our land."

Jesse paused for a couple of minutes as he looked from one end of the empty area beyond to the other end, and as far into the distance as his eyes could see. Finally he turned to his friend, the Flathead Chief. "White men are greedy for land. In California where I had my ranch, small wars were fought over land. The men I sent to the other side burned my ranch, and killed my friends, and they did it all so they could have my land. I fear white men have seen something in your land they want, and will do anything to have it."

Three days later Jesse headed toward Fort Connah. When he arrived and asked if the General was inside, the men smiled, "Hey Gen'l, someone here to see you."

A thunderous voice, thick in Scottish brogue, boomed out the open doorway. "Well tell him to come in lad, or is it a her?"

When Jesse stepped in and moved to the crude wooden desk, a huge man with red hair and beard stood and offered his hand. "Angus McDonald."

"Jesse McKannah."

"Aye lad, it's the old country y'be from is it?"

"No," Jesse answered, "my father Sean came from Ireland before I was born."

"Well lad, a pity it is not to be born in Scotland, but it's better bein' born here than in Ireland to starve to death."

Jesse ignored the slur against his father's home country and looked hard at the huge robust Scotsman. "I've come here with a group of Salish Indians from the western lands to hunt buffalo. What in God's name happened to all of them?"

Rick Magers

"God had nothing to do with it, lad." The Scot looked Jesse straight in the eyes, "Those politicians back east got together and decided to acquire these lands. My wife's Nez Perce, and her people want nothing to do with any kind of deal; likewise the Blackfoot." He pulled open an old wooden drawer and asked Jesse if he'd like a drink of good Scots whiskey.

"Thanks anyway; don't use it."

Angus mumbled, "Hmmm."

"About all those buffalo?"

"Well, some of the Indians wanted to deal with those government skunks, but most said no. One of those bright gov'ment boys had been here before and knew how much these people depend on buffalo. He returned to Washington and told 'em to send trainloads of sport-shooters to kill the buffalo so the Indians would have to deal. At first they killed the buffalo and left 'em to rot. Another smart feller learned that buffalo bones made great fertilizer, so they started killing more'n ever, for the bones. They'd kill 'em, then others would come along and cut out the tongue n' salt it down to carry back east to them fancy new restaurants. Most of the rest of the animal rotted back into the ground. Sorriest bunch o' bastards I've ever seen." He drained the cup and refilled it, "And lad, it was all designed by our own new gov'ment."

Angus McDonald opened the drawer again and filled his tin cup, then looked up at Jesse. "A dispatch arrived last week saying that a wagon train was heading here with supplies for the local Indians?"

Jesse walked to the wall and sat in a huge home built chair. "Did it state what was on it?"

"Food n' everything they'll need to get through the winter, but I wouldn't quit diggin' bitterroot 'till whatever it is gets 'ere. Those politicians' idea of food might be a long way from what we consider eatin' stuff, and Christ 'imself only knows what 'everything they'll need to get through the winter' might mean."

"The Indians say you told them before that there would be supplies, but they have never received anything."

"A month ago a message from a passing trapper stated that a supply train for the Indians was on its way. If it gets here I'll pass it out, but I keep telling them to dig plenty of cama and bitterroot."

"So what d'you think'll be the outcome?" Jesse asked; starting to like the loud, robust Scotsman.

"Pre-determined long ago. Blackfoot and maybe Nez Perce'll hold out and probably die fightin' rather than give in. The rest will no doubt eventually give the gov'ment their land, and sit on a reservation and wait to die…while eating white man's food and drinking white man's whiskey."

"For the life of me, Mister McDonald, I can't imagine anyone killing so many buffalo in such a short time."

"Just Angus, lad, never been a mister in m'life. I've 'eard it said many times; courageous buffalo hunters." Another cup full and he continued. "These Indians could be called that, because they often ride inside the herd to make enough kills, but those," he dramatically emphasized the next four words, "**great American buffalo hunters** are a disgusting bunch of egotistical misfits. Do you know what a buffalo does when you shoot 'im?"

Jesse nodded no. "Drops dead 'e does, 'cause they're easy to kill. Thousands standin' around and a few just lookin' down at 'im. Pow! Another drops. Pow! Another, and another till they're all layin' there on the plains dead." He drank half of the whiskey before adding, "Guess what the Great Buffalo Hunters do next?"

"Go find another herd."

"Yep! You got it lad. Did it for months, day-in n' day-out…boom-boom-boom. They had a motto, 'a dead buffalo is a dead Indian.' I'll bet history's gonna make heroes and great men outa those dregs o' mankind."

● ● ●

Two days after the Blackfoot attacked and burned the expected supply train, and also killed the men bringing it; a pair of young men heading for Great Falls, Montana came upon the charred remains. When they saw the condition of the bodies, wagons, barrels, and crates that had PROPERTY OF THE US GOVERNMENT stamped on the ones that didn't completely burn, the two men changed plans and headed south toward Missoula. The Montana town and mission were almost as far as Great Falls, but the trail to their original destination was through Blackfoot country. The various Salish tribes, who were friendly with white men, controlled the land between them and Missoula.

"Them Blackfoot're on the warpath again," were the first words out when they arrived at Father Pierre-Jean de Smet's mission. After listening, he asked if they would go to Fort Connah, and talk to his friend Angus McDonald.

They agreed to go, and left at once, covering the sixty miles in good time. Jesse was back at the trading post when the two young men arrived with news about the supply wagon train massacre.

Before beginning, Elwood Waggoner looked at the small group of little log buildings. "I thought this was an army post?"

"Yeah," Bevus Pooster chimed in, "how come they call this a fort?" He looked around, "Don't look like no fort I've ever seen."

Angus McDonald seldom tolerated senseless chatter, especially from fools like the two standing before him, but he had just received two cases of Scottish whiskey, and was in a particularly good mood. "Don't know m'self how it come to be called a Fort. Neil McArthur started this place for the Hudson Bay Trading Company in forty-six, then I took over two years later. I named it Connen after a river back in the old country, but Francois Finlay there," he pointed to a small Indian sitting on a huge barrel of brine pickles, "couldn't pronounce it. He called it Connah, so that's what everybody else has called it since. Been that till now n' probably will till it's gone."

"Well you better start makin' it a Fort, 'cause we got us another war on our hands." Elwood was excited and strung his words together. Both men had a difficult time understanding him.

"A war?" Jesse asked.

"Yep," Bevus answered in his long easy drawl, "dang Blackfoot're on the warpath again."

• • •

"Ghost horses," the old Chief said later, when Jesse finished telling him about the incident at Big Salmon Lake, "frightened men see things not there."

"That's what I figured, probably just a small renegade band instead of the big war party those men claimed were on a hundred horses."

"Why would Blackfoot burn wagons with supplies they could take to their camp?"

"Puzzles me too Chief, so me n' Lame Wolverine are going to the lake and look for ourselves."

"Yes! Now I must call a meeting with the Chiefs so they can tell their people that no supplies are coming."

Rick Magers

Jesse and Lame Wolverine moved cautiously through Blackfoot country. When they arrived at the site of the massacre, they could easily see that the Blackfoot set the wagons on fire before leaving, and took the horses back to camp. Crates of thin blankets had been busted open, and material that wasn't consumed by fire was still there.

"Look at this." Lame Wolverine held up a large piece of blanket.

Jesse took one corner of the thin material his friend was holding, and stretched it out. "I can see why they didn't take these with them."

"I wonder what kind of food was in the barrels?"

"I found scraps of buffalo hide." Jesse shook his head, "any food wouldn't have been better quality than these blankets."

That night, after being informed that no supplies would come to help his people survive the winter, the local Chief began his story. "White men began killing buffalo after you were last here. The smell was so bad we could not sleep. We moved away, but dead buffalo lay everywhere. We soon noticed that buffalo were not plentiful, so on a round moon we ran a small herd over a cliff to prepare for winter. White soldiers took us to the fort and put us in little rooms with iron sticks on the windows. The round moon returned and they let us out. They said running buffalo over a cliff was not right. All who were caught doing it would be hung from the neck for breaking white mans law.

Jesse asked, "The White Chief has not sent anything to help you through the winters?"

"No, and I do not think he will until we give him our land."

A young Chief said, "The Blackfoot still do not let white men on their land without war, so the white men do not go there."

• • •

The following day, Jesse's eyes scanned the barren plateaus ahead before looking up toward heaven. "*God,*" he said to himself, "*are these people not also your children?*" He turned his horse and headed toward the fort.

Angus was face down on his desk with both arms dangling. Before Jesse could speak, he lifted his wooly red head, and nodded at the young man he had taken a liking to.

Rick Magers

Jesse walked to the window behind Angus's desk. "I'm heading back into the western mountains Angus."

"Kinda figured you would."

"With Prairie Rose gone I can't stand being in camp."

"She was a fine woman, and I guess only God knows why that Blackfoot killed her."

"I figured that out."

"And what answer did you come up with, lad?"

"It was snowing so hard that I let her wear the big coat she made for me. I had been wearing it since it started snowing, and that Blackfoot musta been watching. He thought it was me in the coat."

"Well lad at least you sent him on his way to the happy hunting ground." He looked solemnly at Jesse; wishing he was going to stay in the area. "Reckon you'll be comin' back this way?"

"I probably will," Jesse answered, "but I gotta get over thinkin' about Rose all the time, and being alone's the only way for me to do it."

Angus turned and walked to the old wooden cabinet where he kept papers and other important documents. After retrieving something, he turned and walked to Jesse. Holding out the object he smiled at the young man, "here, take this with you."

Jesse looked at the beautiful leather holster and ammunition belt holding one of Colt's latest revolvers. He looked up into Angus' grinning face, and then back to the holster.

"Try it on, lad."

Jesse tried to speak but a lump in his throat prevented it. He unwound the cartridge belt and swung it around his hips. With the silver buckle secured, he removed the pistol. Fearing that tears would come into his eyes, he didn't look at the old Scott. After opening the cylinder he slowly removed bullets from the belt one-by-one and filled it. Replacing the loaded weapon into the holster, Jesse carefully removed it twice to aim down the long barrel. Still avoiding Angus' eyes, he said, "What a pistol. This gun is balanced better than any I've ever held." He finally looked at the old man and held out his hand. "Thank you Angus. This is a gift that will never be bettered in my lifetime."

"A better man never wore one, lad, and it's proud I am to have known you."

Rick Magers

Neither man could have guessed that one day an older Jesse would return with his four brothers to right-a-wrong committed against the Flathead Indians. The 44 Colt that Angus McDonald gave him would still be hanging on Jesse McKannah's hip, even though the man who gave it to him would be gone.

THE END

Read

THE McKANNAHS

A western novel

By

Rick Magers

www.grizzlybookz.com

Rick Magers

3

WOO LEE CHONG

~ A Forgotten Western Legend ~

How can he be a legend? I've been asked that same question many times by people in the audience who say they've never heard of him. I ask them if they've heard of Elmer Podandy or Childer Rhumpuss? They invariably answer "no" and then I ask the rest of the audience the same question, and they admit that they have also never heard of any of these three extraordinary western legends. "That's why I'm here," I announce, "to tell you about an incredible young man from China who left an indelible mark on the western frontier of America."

But first let me tell you a little about myself, so you'll understand how I happened across this story. Most of you noticed, I'm sure, that my posters simply state Lecture by an American West Historian. My name is Woo Lee Chong II. Odd name, you wonder, for a round-eyed white man.

Well, that all came about when I began researching our family heritage for my doctorate, and guess who fell out of the family tree? Yep! You guessed it…ole Woo Lee Chong himself.

I was born in 1935 and named Chester Jeremiah Overholster. I was looking forward to climbing my family tree, because I always figured there must be some real characters in it for me to wind up with a name like that. Nope! Just a bunch of plain ole folks—until that is, I got to great-great-grandma.

We'll get to her in awhile, but first let me shake the tree for you. My mama was born in 1900 and was named Mary-Smythe Louella Hampton. She married Omar Bander Overholster in 1920, and then had her one-and-only offspring fifteen years later—me. Mama was always very slow and cautious about everything she did. Her careful, precise methods worked out good for her, because she became a very successful businesswoman during an era when few women left the home to join America's work force.

I always wondered how it worked out for papa, though. After fifteen years—one kid? Mama never struck me as a person who considered the bedroom as a place to do anything except sleep to prepare for another day at the office. As an old saying goes, *you made your bed so lie in it—alone.*

My grandpa was born in 1885 and was named Jeremiah Smythe Hampton, and as you can see, mama didn't get her slow careful ways from her daddy. Mama was born fifteen years after her daddy was born. It was no surprise to me when I finally dug up an old photo of grandma when she was young. Wow! She was one gorgeous hunk, and it even showed through all of those clothes women wore to be photographed back then.

Now we're getting back to that slow and careful bunch again. Grandpa's mama was born in 1850 and named Louella Ella Hampton, so that made her thirty-five when grandpa popped out. I guess great-grandpa was a patient guy like my own papa…genetics? Probably!

Great-great grandma was born in 1810 and named Rebecca Isabel Smythe, and as I said, she had Great-Grandma Louella in 1850. Seems like we're back to that slow and careful side of my family, doesn't it? Wrong! Here's where ole Woo Lee steps out on a limb of the tree.

Great-Great Grandma Smythe was born into a fishing family on the west coast of California, not far from present day San Francisco. From notes that I located in our family Bible, she never took to fishing for a living, and didn't like anything about the ocean. When she was fifteen she talked a spinster aunt who owned a small laundry in Buena Vista—later to be re-named San Francisco—into allowing her to come

Rick Magers

and live with her. I'm quite certain that her family, which was struggling to provide for their thirteen kids, didn't mind seeing one of them leave the nest—especially one that didn't go out in the boat or clean and dress the fish when the catch came in. One less neck to be shoving what little food they had down.

There are plenty of notations in Aunt Maryllyn's Bible, which makes it plain that she cared a lot for her spunky niece. Running from the boonies of what is now Monterey, to avoid a life of drudgery aboard the family fishing vessels, is exactly what Maryllyn Smythe had done herself as a teenager.

At sixteen Great-Grandma Rebecca was too old to return to school, so she went to work in Aunt Maryllyn's laundry. That was where she met Chen Tzu Chong. Starting to get the picture, now? Chen Tzu Chong—Woo Lee Chong. Yep! Chen was to become Woo Lee's daddy.

Chen was in his mid twenties as far as my research determined, and had arrived from Mainland China with his entire family while still very young. He quickly mastered the English language and proved to be a diligent and trusted worker. There are several entries in her Bible where Aunt Maryllyn refers to Chen as; *the yellow glue that binds this motley bunch of chinks together.*

Aunt Maryllyn had to be a tough cookie to have worked herself into her position without the assistance of a man. It's not a big deal today, but back then it was very much a man's world, and most women were up a creek without a paddle if they didn't have a man, or had one and lost him along the way. I never located any mention of a man in her life, so as I stated—tough cookie.

Aunt Maryllyn paid her help, all of which were Chinese with the single exception of her niece, very good for the standard of those days. Each worker received living quarters in her huge rooming house, plus a good healthy breakfast prepared by her Chinese housekeeper, and they were allowed to grow their own vegetables on an acre of fertile land behind the rooming house. Each worker was paid a starting wage of one dollar each week, but could double that within a year if they were industrious. What encouraged them to work hard for Auntie, as they referred to her, was having every Sunday off. It was common during this time for every Chinese worker to devote seven days a week to his or her employer. Aunt Maryllyn's employee turnover rate was zero.

Rick Magers

Soon after beginning to work for Aunt Maryllyn, Chen Tzu was promoted to foreman. Since Great-Grandma Rebecca was working right there with him, it was natural for her to try hard to get along with Chen Tzu, and try to better her position at the laundry. He must have been a good looking man, because even though Aunt Maryllyn never said as much in her notations, (I doubt she cared much for men in general) she did state once that he made an impressive figure standing a full head taller that the rest as he surveyed the operation of her establishment.

It appears as though everything went along with little change for the next couple of years, but then Aunt Maryllyn became suddenly ill with what appears to have been the flu…within days she died.

That woman was always full of surprises, but the one she left behind topped them all. She had never mentioned her will to anyone in the family, so when it was found and read they were all shocked. Everything was left to her niece and Chen Tzu—with stipulations. They had to occupy her big house, which sat in front of her rooming house, and they were to share the duties of running the laundry. If either one decided not to participate, then the entire parcel was to be sold and the money given to a local charity; referred to as Orphans of the Waterfront.

Both being very sensible people, Rebecca and Chen Tzu moved into the house and began sharing the responsibilities of running the laundry. It wasn't long before they began sharing other things in the house. Northern California nights get mighty cold, especially if you're in a bed alone, and before long, Woo Lee Chong was pulled from between Rebecca's legs by the housekeeper, who as notes found later indicate, was also the local midwife who delivered over one-thousand children—all Chinese. She had amassed quite a fortune by the time she died at one-hundred-and-seven.

It became obvious that Woo Lee had not inherited his daddy's height. Several notations in the laundry journal, that Rebecca began when she took over the bookkeeping, mentions several places where young Woo Lee was kept during working hours. He spent his first several months in one of those oblong egg baskets made of thin wooden slats, then was moved to larger quarters—a high-sided wooden wash tub. He must have been about a year old when he began climbing out of the egg basket.

Rick Magers

Woo Lee began working at the laundry as soon as he was old enough to carry a basket full of freshly washed clothes to the people who hung them up to dry. He was only five-years-old it seems. Being too short to hang clothes, he was bent over a tub washing clothes by the time he was ten, and by thirteen he was carrying a basket of finished clothed across town to the customer and returning with the basket filled with soiled clothes.

There was little mentioned about Woo Lee's activities during his younger years, with the exception of his regular Sunday visits to his grandfather. Mao Fu Chong was a Martial Arts Master and saw something in his grandson that others had missed. From the moment Woo Lee had watched Poppy Mao, as he called him at age two and ever after, teaching older boys, he was mesmerized at how effortlessly the small man sent his students to the mat.

By Woo Lee's fourteenth birthday he was unbeatable by everyone except Poppy Mao, and all knew that he could defeat the old man if wanted to. Chen Tzu was very proud of his son's abilities in the revered martial arts. Rebecca knew nothing about martial arts, but made a notation about her small son's ability to 'take down' all of the young men who practiced behind the house every Sunday.

On Woo Lee Chong's sixteenth birthday he was presented with a sets of nunchuks that his grandfather had carved from walrus tusk ivory. The old man had spent a year carving into them the entire story of his grandson's journey during his ancestral passage into a spiritual state of existence; stepping up onto a plateau above mortal men. Woo Lee had achieved a degree of mastery in martial arts that few men ever attain before the age of fifty.

• • •

When the discovery of gold at Sutter's Mill, but a short distance away, reached Woo Lee; he notified his parents and grandfather that he was going there to seek his fortune. The words 'gold discovered' sent tremors throughout the financial world. Other tremors would soon be felt when a short, handsome young Chinaman arrived in Sutter's Mill to take his place among other men eager to stake their claim to fame and fortune.

The first came the day he walked into the boomtown. His clothes were fairly clean; allowing for the trip. He had a look of peaceful unawareness and he was small. These were all good signs to the dregs that are always lurking in the shadows near prosperity.

The resulting court account states that a tall, emaciated man, still reeking of liquor when he was taken to a doctor the following day, lunged from the darkness of a deep doorway to grab the little Chinaman. One witness stated that he saw the tall man's head and feet change places twice in mid-air as he was hurtled across the alley. A second witness said that even drunk, the man's instincts brought him to his feet, which was a mistake. He said the small Chinaman was flying through the air 'like a cat going over a tall fence with a dog at its heels'…apparently Woo Lee landed and struck at the same time. The first witness said, "I got real close 'cause I wanted to know how many arms that little Chinaman had. Looked t'me like he had three on each side that hit that thievin' drunk afore he had sense enough to fall down, and stay down."

Another account stated that three days later Woo Lee rescued a dog from a bully who was abusing it. Because the man was severely injured by Woo Lee there was an inquest to find out what led up to it. Witnesses stated that the man had the dog on a short rope and was beating it with a thick stick. Woo heard the dog screaming and ran into the alley, then threw the man aside and stationed himself between the man and the dog.

The man swung the stick at Woo Lee, who jumped nimbly aside, and then produced two short ropes so swiftly that none of the several witnesses who had gathered could explain where they came from. One witness described for the court what happened next. "There was a chunk of white wood or som'n at both ends of two short ropes and that little Chinaman was swinging them so fast that a feller couldn't hardly see 'em. He slowly approached that big feller there," he apparently pointed at the man who had been abusing the dog.

Everyone in the courtroom, which was the main dining room of a hastily built restaurant, turned to look at the man. He was described in the court record as six-foot-six-inches and weighing about three hundred pounds. It was also noted that he had many stitches closing wounds on his head, face, and neck.

The witness continued, "That little Chinaman told the feller to stop beating the dog and leave the alley, but he was infuriated at that little Chinaman swinging a toy of some kind in his face. That big fella lunged at the Chinaman with his stick all drawed back for a death blow, but the Chinaman just stepped aside, and faster'n yallerjackets can come outa the ground and swarm ya, he struck that bully with them little white things on the ends of the ropes so many times that he was lyin' there either unconscious or smart enough to act like he was."

It wasn't the first time that the bully had singled out someone or something smaller to vent his rage on, so all of the witnesses were on Woo Lee's side and testified on his behalf, which resulted in him being cleared of any wrong doing. The bully was tossed into jail for thirty days as a habitual nuisance and fined fifty dollars court costs and told to pay the doctor's bill of thirty-five dollars before leaving his cell—and the town.

Woo Lee Chong did what almost every person who came to Sutter's Mill did. He dug his heart out trying to strike it rich, but when the gold started petering out he found that he only had enough money left to head back home and see how his parents were doing.

Back then as now, a lot can happen in a year. When he arrived home he was informed that Chen Tzu had died not long after Woo Lee had left for Sutter's Mill, and his grandfather, Poppy Mao had returned to China with the rest of the Chong family. Woo Lee Chong's mother, Rebecca, had sold the laundry and moved back to Monterey. She later married Rupert Elijah Hampton and gave birth to a daughter when she was forty years old that she named Louella.

Woo Lee still had traveling dust in his shoes, so he began looking for a job that would allow him to see more of the country that he was born in. He eventually landed one with the Overland Stage Company as a traveling porter. He rode standing on the rear, or if space allowed, sitting on top with the passenger's baggage. When a passenger departed, Woo Lee (Wooly as he was called by company employees) handed their luggage down and then carried it into the hotel for them.

Due to his personality, which was described as dynamic and full of self-confidence, he was eventually promoted to guard, and was then sitting next to the driver; holding a shotgun almost as long as he was tall.

Woo Lee knew that the shotgun made the passengers feel safer, but he knew that his true weapons were hanging down from the back of his neck and resting on his chest beneath the loose fitting rawhide shirt.

Wooly's reputation began the day that the stage was stopped by two bandits. He complied when told to drop the shotgun and climb down with the key to unlock the safe, which was attached to the coach's frame. The driver handed Wooly the key and remained in the seat with his foot on the brake. An elderly passenger traveling to Deadwood, in Dakota Territory made the following statement for the sheriff the following day. "As soon as that little Chinaman's feet touched ground, both bandit's guns were knocked from their hands by what appeared to be a flock of white birds attacking them, but were actually some kind of weapon Wooly had in his hands."

The two bandits were so badly injured that one died on the way to Deadwood, and the other became the town idiot. Little ole Woo Lee Chong was making a reputation for himself.

I could go on and on about the many events that shaped Woo Lee Chong's life in the west, but I'm allowed only so much time to speak to each audience before turning the stage over to my traveling co-host. I'll end by telling you about the most famous encounter that he had, even though his name has never been recorded as a participant on that infamous day.

Most of us have followed the exploits of the men who helped tame the Wild West. James Butler Hickok was certainly one, and became famous as Wild Bill. In the early days before becoming sheriff, he was employed by the Overland Stage Company.

A gang of bandits were operating out of Rock Creek, Nebraska and had robbed so many of their stage's passengers, plus had taken the money being shipped in their safes, that they hired Wild Bill Hickok to put a stop to it.

As often happens, fate put Woo Lee Chong there in Rock Creek that day. After proving that he could handle the team of horses, Wooly was promoted to driver. His regular run would include Rock Creek; so on the day that attacking would confront the gang, Woo Lee was pulling into town for the first time.

For those of you who haven't kept up with the facts of this encounter, the gang was known as The McCandles Boys, but boys they were not. These were hardened desperadoes who would kill in a heartbeat.

History has recorded it as just another of Wild Bill Hickok's adventures. Supposedly he took on the entire gang single-handedly and after killing three of them the rest left and never returned. That account is understandable when you consider the name he was making for himself with help from the publishers of dime novels flooding the market in eastern cities. Wild Bill might not have cared, but those book publishers certainly didn't want their western hero sharing their lucrative spotlight with a five-foot-tall Chinaman.

When you read all of the reports as I did, another scenario develops. Just before the McCandles Boys showed up in Rock Creek, Wooly was pulling into town with his stagecoach. After seeing to it that his passengers were taken care of, he headed toward the livery to ask that his team of horses be changed.

The confrontation between The McCandles Boys and Wild Bill took only ten minutes, and when it was over one of the McCandles Boys had a bullet hole in his heart, but the other two had broken necks and so many broken bones and bruises, that it was determined that the horses inside the corral where they were shooting from had stampeded and trampled them to death.

A witness later stated that he had seen a small man removing something from around his neck while sneaking toward the two McCandles brothers.

Soooooo, James Butler Hickok became a legend as Wild Bill Hickok and Woo Lee Chong has remained anonymous all these years.

I figured that any relative of mine with that kind of true grit should be remembered, so I legally changed my name to Woo Lee Chong II and he has become a legend in my family.

If the opportunity ever presents itself, dig through your family's past, because you never know who might fall out of one of those trees.

THE END

Rick Magers

4

THE LONE RANGER

He was tall, muscular, and lean...common for a man who had spent many of his 40 years roaming the barren Texas/Mexican border. He was also as black as black gets before turning to an almost iridescent purple. When the Civil War ended, Joshua was a free man. His service record as an infantry soldier, and later as a Buffalo Soldier with the cavalry, was exceptional. He fought the Apache with the same fierce determination that he had when fighting the Confederacy prior to volunteering for the newly organized Corp of Buffalo Soldiers.

The only close friend he made during his time with the cavalry was a mounted soldier named Ledford, who once commented, "Josh, you scares me when I sees you charging ahead right into them crazy damn crackers. What make you so wild like dat, boy?"

"Ain no man got no right to make annuder man do his work for him as a slave, Led, like dem crackers do. Dey juss ain no reason folks oughta be killin all de hard working folks what juss tryin to git along. Ain no reason eeduh why black and white folks caint git along on dis eart. Lawd knows de hard ole groun make life hard enuff without all de raidin an killin."

"Yeah! Seem t'me dey plenty room fo every kinda folks dey is to fine someplace what to live on an be leff alone."

Rick Magers

"They is, Led, they is. Juss too many greedy fella what want all de lan fo themselfs an they own folks, an dem crackers want udder folks do all de hard work."

Joshua still felt the same about one group of people treating another group like slaves, but he seldom expressed his inner feelings to others. His friend Ledford was the only person he ever revealed his feelings about anything to, and when a Confederate officer shoved a sword through Led, Josh decided to form no more close bonds with anyone. He had changed in other ways too. He listened to those around him speak and slowly removed all of the slave slang he was taught as a child on a North Carolina tobacco plantation as a slave's son.

At thirteen he had been working sixteen-hour days, seven days a week since he turned ten. He decided to either escape or die trying, but told nobody, not even his parents and siblings.

Returned escapees, who survived the whipping, brought valuable information back to the slave community. There were people outside who were organizing underground routes where escaped slaves could get assistance to go north—if they could just make it to them. The returned slaves brought with them the locations of these places and shared them with their fellow slaves.

Only a few days prior to Josh's 14th birthday, the November weather was perfect for his plan. Fog had been almost clinging to the ground for two days and there was no breeze at all. He had stolen pepper from the storeroom on the days he was called to unload wagonloads of supplies.

His aunt Tanni had lectured he and all of his sisters and brothers about which local plants were edible and which were poisonous. At every opportunity when on a detail in the woods, he picked the poison plants and hid them within his clothing. Back in the camp he would dry them, using extreme caution not to be seen. Two years later he had a sufficient quantity of pepper and the poisonous dried leaves to fit his escape plan.

Josh knew he would need all of the head start possible, but also realized that he must wait until everyone in both his camp, and the master's mansion, was asleep for the night.

• • •

By midnight he had been silently walking for an hour toward the place where the summer sun always set…and he could still hear the dogs in the kennels. He was taking no chance that someone would awaken and hear him running. When the dogs could no longer be heard, he began a paced run that would put him as far away from the plantation and the dogs as possible, by the time the trackers came after him.

He knew that the master's two trackers and their six bloodhounds would be on his trail as soon as they awakened and realized he was gone.

Since he was very young, Joshua had set traps in the woods far away from the houses and checked them at night. They supplied his family with enough extra food to survive the meager rations doled out by the master's head foreman. After the foreman stole a share from each slave household, there was barely enough left to take the nagging edge off of their constant hunger.

Josh stopped running and cut the three rabbits in half with a stolen kitchen knife. He knew both slave trackers would have three dogs, because he'd seen them leave many times in pursuit of slaves who could no longer stand the abuse. He had used a stone during the past weeks to almost silently get the blade sharp. He now slit open the meat in several places. All was accomplished by feel, as it was a pitch-black night with fog so thick that he probably couldn't have seen his hands and the rabbit parts anyway. Into the slits he shoved the finely ground poison leaves. He then separated the skin from the carcass in places and did the same. Afterward, he carefully spread the deadly meat across the ground where he felt certain the dogs, that seemed as starved as the slaves, could not refuse. He prayed that the trackers could not see what the dogs were going to and would allow them to go individually to the six different chunks of poisoned meat.

He resumed his journey toward the coast where people against slavery would help him escape to the north aboard a ship.

As dawn began peeking through the thick layer of fog, which still hid him from potentially hostile eyes, he felt flames going down his throat to burn his lungs—still he did not slow his pace but once, and then only long enough to walk slowly for a half hour to spread the pepper. He was told that if the poison didn't slow down the hounds, the pepper might throw them off the trail long enough for a slave to find help and escape to the north.

Rick Magers

He was correct about the dogs. Six lay gasping and groaning on the ground behind him…temporarily worthless as tracking dogs.

● ● ●

Sixteen days later, a freezing and starving Joshua lay silently watching a house on the outskirts of a small village named Lindle. If a slave let it be known that he could read or write, or worse yet do both, his life was in jeopardy. Joshua was obviously bright, and had been taught to read and write by the plantation owner's kindly wife, who secretly detested slavery. So when he cautiously approached the sign in the pre-dawn light, he knew he was in the right place. He had never seen the ocean and could not even imagine what it must look like, but he knew that what he smelled was it. *I am near the sea—freedom soon. Thank you, dear Lord, for guiding my feet.*

Summoning more courage than most men ever have need of, Josh approached the house at as close to midnight as he could judge. He searched in the dark until he located the cellar door, and rapped three times, paused and then rapped five more times. Finally a ground level window opened and a voice called softly, "What do you want?"

His answer was exactly what his escaped uncle told him before dying of his infected whipping wounds. "A free parrot and a dead cracker."

Moments later the cellar door opened so silently that he was startled when a woman's voice said, "Come with me" as a gentle hand touched his shoulder.

Trembling from fright and the freezing cold, he allowed her to lead him into the warmth of the dark cellar. His eyes could not pick up so much as a slight variation in the blackness of the room, but he dutifully allowed his savior to lead him to the Promised Land. He had no idea how she moved so swiftly through the blackness and was not surprised when he later learned that she owned the house and had been blind since birth.

A week later, as he prepared to board a ship at night, which would take him to Boston Harbor, his benefactor held his arm and reached to his hand. Squeezing it she said something that remained with him all his life. "I have been forced to live my life in darkness, but you have a bright world out there waiting for you, so never be afraid to help another soul foundering in the darkness of distress and despair."

• • •

Joshua entered the small Mexican village of el Centro long after dark. Earlier he had ground-tethered his horse near a stand of trees and sat with his back against a tree, silently watching the town through a small folding telescope.

Four hours later, with eyes sore from watching ten villages in as many days, he was about to leave for his next destination, when he suddenly tensed. He leaned away from the tree as though he could see the two men better. He swung the telescope from one man to the other until he spotted what he had searched for during the past year and a half.

The short man was nearest to him, which offered a perfect view. Josh concentrated on the little man's left leg as he walked toward the cantina porch. His limp was exaggerated even with the odd three-inch lift attached to the sole and heel of his boot.

The muscles in Joshua's jaw flexed as he watched the fat man join the short one and enter the cantina. *Took a long time boys, but I found you. Enjoy the drinks, because they'll be your last.*

Joshua Harding had been recommended by Colonel Bolder T. Asterman, his commanding officer during the Civil War, and also by Captain James P. Handle the officer in charge of the Buffalo Soldiers. Josh carried letters from both men when he walked into the office of the Texas Rangers.

Colonel Banenfield was surprised to see a black man enter his office. He was deadset against all aspects of slavery and didn't have a prejudiced thought in his head, but a black had never entered before.

"Colonel Banenfield, sir," Joshua began, "my commanding officer is a friend of yours, and suggested that I talk to you about becoming a Texas Ranger. Josh stood at attention until the man seated behind the desk spoke.

"At ease soldier, the war's over." Josh spread his feet and placed his hands behind his back and remained rigid, and his eyes never left the colonel—and they never blinked.

The man read both letters of recommendation, and Josh noticed that he too never once blinked. He was also a man who did not want to miss anything. Without saying a word, he opened a drawer in his desk and brought out a letter and held it out. "This came in the stagecoach's mailbag a month ago. Go ahead and read it."

After reading the letter, Josh handed it back. "They're both very good men, sir, and it was an honor to serve under them.

"You must be one helluva good tracker to get in n' outa that many Apache camps without ending up roasting over a fire."

"My mama was a full blood Cherokee and taught me a lot, sir."

"How'd you end up a slave with an Indian mother?"

"Daddy escaped from a Georgia cotton plantation and was taken in by a Cherokee tribe in the mountains when he was still just a boy. Some slave trackers caught him and mama alone trailing a bear he shot, and took them both to the tobacco plantation that the trackers worked for. That's where I was born."

"I see here that you enlisted at sixteen as soon as you arrived in Massachusetts."

"Yessir! I had very little experience at doing anything, so I figured the army would teach me a lot."

"And did they?"

"Yessir, they sure did."

"And what do you consider the most useful?"

"To follow orders."

Josh liked it that the man listened intently to every word. His gray head shook slowly up and down as he spoke. "Sometimes a man must do and say things that he normally wouldn't to make his way in this world." He paused and looked at Josh for a full minute. Josh locked eyes with the man and never blinked or looked away—nor did the colonel.

The Ranger chief finally took his lower lip between the thumb and forefinger of his left hand and squeezed his lips in thought a moment. "Joshua, I've had a plan for quite some time, but haven't met anyone that I thought could handle it," He grinned, "until now."

• • •

For the next twenty years, Joshua worked as an undercover Texas Ranger. He patrolled the Texas/Mexican border intercepting hundreds of criminals who were trying to get into Mexico to disappear. He was at home in the wilderness and was accepted by both Mexicans and Indians who lived near the Rio Grande.

While tracking a stagecoach bandit who had killed the driver, his shotgun guard, and the two passengers, Joshua silently entered a Kawevikopaya Yavapai Indian camp. They're often referred to as Tonto Apache, and will fight when they must, but prefer to lead a peaceful life. He stood rigidly upright as he walked ahead of his horse along the path between the mud, straw, and stick huts. He knew the chief's large hut would be in the center of the others, because he had entered many of their camps, but never this one. Squaws looked up disinterested as he passed, and young braves stopped what they were doing and watched with cautious eyes. Josh stopped his horse at the chief's hut and spoke in their language. *I have come to ask for the chief's help.*

A man as tall as Josh came through the flap, followed by three young braves. He was almost as black as Josh, but had long black Indian hair as straight as any Josh had seen. It was secured to his head by a rattlesnake-skin band.

Josh spoke slowly and respectfully in the man's own language. *I am searching for two bandits. One is a very bad man and has killed everyone he's robbed for no reason. One eye is missing and he often wears a patch. He also has a bad leg and limps.*

The tall Indian shook his head slowly up and down then answered. "I learned my father's language, so if it easier for you, speak in your own tongue."

"Thank you, chief. Even after many years along the Rio Grande there are still many words in your tongue that I do not know."

"Come into my home and smoke with me and my sons. Men should only kill other men in battle and then only when there is no other way. We will help you if we can."

The chief told Josh that the man had been in the area but moved on when he realized he was being watched. "That was only two days ago, so I will send two of my best trackers to see which way he is heading, and then you will know where to go. This will save you much time and you can rest to be ready to go after him."

Rick Magers

The chief said that it would soon be dark and the tracks would be very hard for him to follow, and suggested that he stay the night in his village. Weariness had descended upon Josh during the last couple of days, so he accepted the chief's offer…it would change his life.

The fire felt good on Josh's chilled body, and the hot bowl of puma stew was the best meal he had tasted in months. The chief explained, "My his father was an African Negro who survived a sinking slave ship, and floated on a hatch cover to the Mexican coast. He was befriended by English missionaries, who taught him to read and write their language, and also taught him many other skills that he used as he aged." The chief smiled at Josh. "His entire life changed the day my mother visited the missionary with her parents. He was a huge man with arms that resembled the trunk of a tree, but he was a very peace loving man. He never bothered anyone unless they angered him beyond his limit. I remember as a child a fight that two of our braves engaged each other in over a young maiden. My father was made chief by that time, and he grabbed each young warrior by the arm to stop their battle, before one hurt the other. He told them, I will settle this now. You will each use a knife and fight until one dies, and then the winner will fight me to the death and I will then have rid this peaceful village of two problems. Is that agreeable to both of you?" The chief looked at Josh and chuckled. "They both said no at the same time. The maiden moved into the hut of an old medicine man and took care of him until he died. The two braves remained good friends until they were killed by raiding Mexican horse thieves."

"Your father was a wise man. Mine was too but the man who owned him was very hard and made him work all of the time."

The chief turned to Josh. "One man should never own another man. Mexican raiders steal our young and sell them in towns far away to be slaves for rich Mexican families."

The chief was silent as he refilled the pipe that the two men had been smoking, when suddenly a young girl entered the hut. "Father, may I sit with you and your friend and listen to the stories?"

The chief patted the fur beside him. "You are always welcome to sit with me when I am not in council with our tribe's elders." He looked toward Josh, "Unless my guest disapproves."

Josh had not taken his eyes off the young girl since she entered the hut. "Oh no, uh no, certainly not, he stammered. When I was a child my father allowed me to sit with him when he spoke to his friends, and I was very proud."

The young maiden leaned forward to speak directly to Josh. "I am not a child. I will have seen seventeen summers and winters next month."

"And you speak perfect English," Josh commented to cover his embarrassment. "Have you been to a missionary school?"

"No! Since I was a child my father has been teaching me to speak his other language." She leaned farther out to continue, "And that was a long time ago, mister…?" She paused a moment because her womanly instincts told her that this black man was very taken with her beauty.

And beautiful she was. Her long black hair hung down on each side in a braid. When Josh later met the chief's wives, he knew immediately which one was her mother. From her father's genes she had inherited not only his dark shiny skin but his strong personality as well, and from her mother—her natural beauty.

She brought Josh out of his temporary stupor by repeating, "Mister…"

"Uh, oh, uh, please forgive me my terrible manners. I have not even introduced myself to your father." He turned to the chief, "Joshua Harding." The chief nodded and said, "I am Wampanahah, and this is," but before he could say his daughter's name, she answered, "Bekkatee." Her father just smiled as she reached out to give Josh her hand, "I am pleased to meet you, Mister Harding."

He shook her delicate hand gently then said, "Josh, please just call me Josh."

"Okay then, Josh it will be, and when you return I will show you the most beautiful meadow next to a small stream that is in this part of the land."

"When I finish my business, Bekkatee, I will return to see your favorite meadow."

"Not Beka'tee, Bek khat' ee." She smiled and waited.

"Bek khat' ee."

"Yes! Your tongue follows our language well."

"I have never been in this village, but I have traveled these trails for a very long time and learned to speak with many different people."

Rick Magers

"I must go now and help my mother." She stood and only then did Josh notice how tall she was. He quickly got his feet beneath him and reached for her hand, wanting to touch her again.

"I look forward to seeing you again." He shook her hand then added, "very soon, I hope."

The chief smiled to himself thinking, *her mother is visiting her sister in the next village. Women know how to keep a man interested if they are interested in him. Daughter has finally met a man to her liking.*

Josh remained in the camp the following day, but never once glimpsed the chief's daughter. Before dawn on the third day, the chief awakened him. "Come, my trackers have returned."

Josh always slept fully dressed, and jumped up to follow the chief. By the time they got to his hut, the chief's wives had the fire burning bright enough to see the drawing the two men made on the dirt floor.

"This is where the two men were when we saw them, and here is where we think they are going."

Josh studied the map before asking in their language; *"this is the big river that runs beside your camp?"*

"Yes!"

"They have doubled back to throw anyone tracking them off their trail." He looked at the trackers and they both shook their head in agreement.

"Thank you very much. I might have missed that." He stood saying, *"I will leave now and will return when they are in chains or dead."*

As he headed his horse out of the camp, the chief turned to his two braves. *"I think the two men will die."* Both shook their heads.

● ● ●

Almost twenty years previously, Josh was sitting beside a stream a short distance from the boundary separating Mexico from Texas.

Colonel Banenfield had not told anyone about Josh, and had gone to the supply room himself and filled Josh's saddlebags with dry beans, a small sack of cornmeal, beef jerky, a slab of cured bacon, and ammunition for the pistol he'd noticed on his new Texas Ranger's hip. As pre-arranged, Josh met him behind the livery stable after dark.

"Joshua, this oughta be enough supplies to keep you going for awhile, and here's ten, ten-dollar gold pieces to buy more when you run out. Those two men I told you about are but a few of the criminals who will be robbing and killing along the border, so they can run into Mexico if necessary. Track 'em as far as you have to, and either kill 'em or bring the bastards back to hang; that'll be up to them. I'll put your thirty-two dollars a month salary in the bottom drawer of my desk with your name and Ranger number inside, in case I get killed or drop dead of bleeding hemorrhoids from sitting on my ass so much these days. You remember where to leave me word when you have to?"

"Yessir! The feedbag nailed higher than the rest will have my new orders in it. When I come here I'll turn that feed bag upside down so you can tell that I've completed an assignment and picked up my new orders. I'll be here waiting for you the following night and every night for a week, in case you've gone off on business. After that, if you still haven't showed I'll come into town the next day and see when you're expected back."

"Right! And if I've been killed, see the new commanding officer and tell him what you've been doing."

"I will, but that'll be after I've tracked down the men who killed you."

It was never necessary, because the colonel was still commanding the Texas Rangers. Many of his men who had hoped to succeed him had quit, died, been killed, or accepted the common notion that he would out-live them all.

• • •

Josh heard a horse whinny, then some splashing as two horses crossed the river not far from where he sat. He had tracked the two men the colonel had told him about, and knew they were in the area where he was waiting. He had trained his horse to remain motionless and silent when Josh grabbed its left ear and cupped the nostrils with his left hand. He released the horse's nose and ear then began to move silently toward the area where he heard voices.

"Git a fire goin' Brandt, and I'll git them saddlebags with the grub in 'em."

Rick Magers

"Yeah man, Louie! Ahm starved near t'death."

Josh moved to within fifty feet and waited. He was a patient man, and knew that a relaxed enemy was easier to take down. One hour later both men had eaten and were leaning back against their saddles lying near the fire. As they passed a bottle of tequila back and forth, Josh smiled. When the bottle was empty and both men had been snoring for an hour, Josh entered their camp as silent as a rattler. A swift lick with the barrel of his Colt revolver and the fat one was out cold. The skinny man heard something and tried to get to his feet while frantically searching for his rifle. It took only a light tap of the barrel to knock the man out. With steel handcuffs on both men, Josh opened their saddlebags and got their coffee beans. After pulverizing enough for his coffee, he scooped them from the flat stone and into the pot of water he'd put on the fire.

While waiting for the coffee to boil, he searched their horses for a rope. Finding a short hemp rope, he cut it in half and tied both men's hands securely behind their back.

Both men regained consciousness and appeared to be over the effects of the quart of tequila. At dawn Josh was preparing them for the two-day journey to the Texas Ranger post.

"Whadaya mean get on m'horse backwards? Ah cain't do thet."

The thin man echoed his partner.

Josh removed his colt from the holster and cocked it. "Very well then, I'll shoot both of you and load your sorry ass across your saddle. Don't matter to me because I get the same bounty dead or alive." That was all the motivation the two men required, because all bandits knew that bounty hunters preferred to take their men in dead, and they had no reason to believe he wasn't a bounty hunter.

"Wait, wait, wait, I kin get up there and turn around in the saddle."

"Yeah, me too."

With both sitting backwards and their hands tied securely to the saddle horn, Josh headed toward Leadville where the colonel's office was positioned inside the Post.

When the town was in sight, Josh spoke for the first time since leaving—he hadn't answered one of their questions. "If I was you, I wouldn't spook these horses because if they run off into the wilderness, the Apache will be happy to get you both down out of those saddles."

Rick Magers

"Hey Colonel Banenfield, lookit what's comin' t'ards town." He came around his desk and onto the porch. When he saw the horses walking slowly into town he knew exactly what had happened. "Take 'em to the jail and get the horses into the livery, 'cause they look starved." When back behind his desk he filled a small glass from the bottle of tequila in the lower drawer of his desk. *And they thought you black folks were too stupid to be soldiers…heh, heh, heh.*

• • •

Josh felt as the two braves did…that the men were going straight for Laredo. As he rode toward the town however, his mind was on Bekkatee. It was almost a fatal error not to be his usual vigilant self.

He arrived on the outskirts of Laredo the next day after dark. It was just a small border village, so he cautiously circled the entire area before entering. Josh silently walked his horse down the alley beside each of the three cantinas. He had been in Laredo several times, posing as a bounty hunter in search of outlaws, so he was familiar with the layout.

He stopped the horse at each window and stood in the stirrups to see into the cantina. After satisfying himself that the men he searched for were not among the customers in any of the three places, he turned and headed toward the livery stable. *I'll rub down Pal and feed him, then go find som'n t'eat m'self. I saw ole Jacarillo that runs the livery, sittin' in Jaime's Cantina, so he won't be back here till tomorrow, and I'll pay him then.*

Half an hour later he went to the rear door of the livery stable and opened it slowly, then stepped into the cool black night. His hand was still on the handle of the door when he felt a terrible blow to the side of his head…and his lights went out.

• • •

Bekkatee entered the hut of her father, Wampanahah and sat beside him. She remained silent, which was unlike her. After several minutes he turned to her. "What is troubling you, daughter?"

"As I watched the black gringo riding away yesterday, I had a vision. I could still see his horse but the man faded away as the dark does when Mother Sun arrives."

The old chief remained silent for a moment before turning to her. "You like this black gringo?"

"Yes! He has kind eyes that do not roam across my body as all of your braves do."

He looked deeply into her coal black eyes and saw deep concern. "I will tell the same two braves who found the men he is searching for to go and see if the black man is okay."

She turned to him and got down on her knees to put her arms around his neck. "You are a good daddy; thank you."

"And you are a good daughter that keeps me feeling young, even though your mother must now chew the tough meat for me. I thank the life spirits often for sending you to me in my old age."

"And my mother thanks them for sending you to her."

"You think so?"

"I know so, father."

• • •

Josh felt as though he had been dropped off a cliff when he began regaining consciousness. He opened his eyes to barely a slit and tried to see where he was without alerting whoever had knocked him out. Everything was blurry, so he closed them tight and waited a moment. The second time, everything was a bit clearer, so he continued opening and closing them. He could now see that he was in a small room and was lying against a wooden wall. He could see everything in the room, so Josh knew he was alone. When he tried to sit up he realized that his hands and feet were tied together behind him. *I must have been daydreaming to let this happen.* He spent long enough trying to loosen the ropes to know they had done a good job of tying him up. He laid his head against the earthen floor and squeezed his eyes shut; exhausted from the effort. His mind wandered back to one of his first assignments. *I think one of these guys mighta been the one I tied to a tree for the Colonel to find.*

As he lay there on the floor, hogtied like a sow waiting to be butchered, his mind wandered back.

•••

Josh had walked casually into the cantina and stood to the side of the batwing doors, allowing his eyes to become adjusted to the dim light. All of the fifty or so Mexicans either took a quick sly look at the tall black man who had just entered, or turned to look directly at him. None had ever seen him, but most had heard stories about the black bounty hunter. The new model Colt, six-shot revolver, hanging in a well-oiled holster on his hip, told them all they needed to know. *Don't give any trouble to this man with eyes that look like two chips of coal on patches of dirty snow against a black mountain.*

Several noticed that he didn't blink once during the ten minutes he stood inside. Without saying a word, he turned and left as silently as he'd entered.

Josh had been alone so many years that he seldom talked, even when with others, and even then his conversation was always limited to specifics—never casual chitchat.

Josh was certain that he was on the trail of the two bandits, and would soon have them. He'd tracked their horses to this small Mexican town a hundred miles south of the Rio Grande. When on a case like this he was given permission, in secret by his commanding officer, Colonel Banenfield, to go as deep into Mexico as he wanted. They had killed a fellow Texas Ranger.

He climbed back on his horse and began circling the village. Even in the waning light of day, no tracks escaped the eyes of Jeremiah. Until recently he had been tracking Apache warriors across some of the most difficult terrain in the west. Satisfied that the two men were in the village, and by now would have been told about his arrival, he headed out of town and then when beyond sight, backtracked toward a small copse of trees a short distance from the village.

At midnight, the bartender locked the rear door of the cantina after stepping out. The round little man had shoved the padlock together and was about to turn when a cold steel blade was placed against his neck. His long Poncho Villa mustache twitched like a frightened cat when a too-calm voice spoke softly. "Where are they?" Jeremiah spoke in perfect Spanish in a deadly tone that made chills run up the man's spine.

The little man answered with one word. "Puta."

Rick Magers

"Stay alive amigo, and take me to the whorehouse."

Josh could hear the two men and what sounded like more than two women talking and laughing. "That dumbass black Texas Ranger slave what's posing as a bounty hunter, couldn't find his own black ass with both hands."

The man laughed and the other added, "Yeah! He headed on outa town toward Ocho Diva, and in a coupla hours when we're finished partying with you gals, we're headin' t'other goddamm way. Ha, haw, haw." Both laughed and the women joined in.

Go on home now, Jeremiah whispered in the bartender's ear, and cover your head with the pillow. The round little man left in a silent rush.

Three hours before dawn, the rear door of the whorehouse opened and three Mexican whores left—their wages earned for the evening.

Josh removed the rawhide tong that secured the Colt to the holster, and lifted the long barreled six shot pistol out, quietly cocking it. He leaned against the wall in the darkness and waited. Jeremiah allowed the men to get on their horses. He knew that in the light of a full moon he could shoot them both from the saddle before they could turn their mounts to make a run for it, and he wanted them silhouetted against a bright sky. His breathing was controlled and unheard, and his gun was held in a steady hand that was ready to strike like a stepped-on rattler.

• • •

Joshua Harding began life as Issana Donodado on the Caribbean island of Trinidad. His mother and father saw the huge slave boats anchoring in the harbor and fled into the hills with the others from their village. This fleet of slave ships was under the command of an ex-pirate who was now employed by a group of southern cotton and tobacco plantations to provide them with slaves. They arrived with hunting hounds and had little trouble locating enough healthy young slaves, including Issana Donodado and his parents. Infants were prize catches because their mothers could breast feed them and they took up very little room. Once they became the property of the plantation, they were trained exactly as the young hounds were—obey the master.

While still an infant, the plantation owner's wife renamed Issana, Joshua Harding. He then became one more in the huge Harding family. There were fifty-seven slaves and they were all named after Jefferson Davis Harding.

From an early age, Josh was a rebel, but he kept it inside. He had seen what happened to those who did not follow the orders of the field boss, and the mansion boss. He obeyed every order and dreamed of freedom.

• • •

The barrel was pointing straight at one of the men when Jeremiah spoke. "Raise your hands or go to Texas lying across your saddles." The warning entered drunken ears. Jeremiah left town at dawn with the two men following on their horses…tied across their saddles—one bullet hole in the chest of each man.

A few days later, the horses with the bodies of the killers lying across their saddles, entered the border town where the Ranger Post and headquarters was temporarily located. The stench of death followed the horses and people turned away. Colonel Banenfield knew exactly who had sent them to town. The dead Ranger's badge was pinned to the corpse of one of the men. *My black lone Ranger is even better than I thought he was.*

• • •

Joshua had been in tight spots before but never this bad. He turned to his other his side and searched every inch of the room that he could see. Rolling back to his other side he thought, *this must be some kinda storeroom or root cellar. I gotta find a…*he stopped in mid-thought as the door opened. Josh closed his eyes and feigned unconsciousness.

"Black Ranger bastard's still out."

"Check his ropes and check 'em good."

The man was pulling on each rope and talking to the other man. "Howja know he was one o' them dang Rangers, instead of a bounty man?"

"Cuz he's the bastard what caught me and tied me to a tree outside o' that damn Ranger town, that's how."

"Wha'd they do to ya?"

"Sent me to Camp Grace over in Hempstead, Texas for three lousy years." Josh heard the man approach and then felt a hard kick in the side. "Stinkin' goddamm Texas Ranger bastard's gonna pay for it now. C'mon, let's go get a bottle of cactus juice and relax till nightfall when we can get his big ass in a wagon and tote him out where nobody ain't gonna hear him scream."

Two hours later they were back. The one who Josh knew was the boss…the bandit he'd caught before he could get into Mexico, held a nearly empty bottle of tequila. "Well, well, niggah boy, awake huh?" He leaned down and almost fell on top of Josh. "Payback time, boy. You're gonna wish you stayed in Texas when I'm done with you." He turned the bottle up and finished the last of the tequila. "C'mon you lazy goddamm Polack, an hep me tote this big black som'bitch out to the wagon."

Josh had noticed that the other man was so drunk that he was leaning against the wall asleep. The empty bottle hit the wall a few inches from his head. The man snapped awake yelling, "What? What! Goddamm, Lute what the hell'd ya do that fer?"

"To'ja t'git aholt of his goddamned legs n' hep me git im in that there goddamm wagon outside."

"Well dammit, y'did'nt hafta waste that damn takeely agin the wall."

"I already drank the cactus you dumbass, Polack."

"That was all we had n' you didn't save me a bit?"

"Relax, I got three bottles stashed in the wagon, you moron, now git aholt an less git him outa here afore the sun comes up."

"I better put that rag over his trap again so's he caint holler."

"Yeah! That's what I jus stole ya t'do."

Two hours later the wagon came to a stop. By the commotion, and what Josh could see, he knew that the one man had fallen off of the wagon seat. The other man was laughing while his partner was trying to get his drunken legs beneath him.

When he was standing, the man growled, "Gimme that goddamm bottle ya stupid Polack." The man drank from the bottle, and tossed it to the man weaving back and forth…about to fall again, and then began laughing. "Em ere cactuses sure mess up a fellers legs." He placed the bottle on the seat, climbed down, and removed the rear gate from the wagon.

"Git aholt o' his laig n' hep me drag his sorry black ass outa there."

Rick Magers

Josh tensed, feeling certain that he was about to hit the ground, but then the one told his pal to stop pulling. He leaned toward Josh, "I'm gonna cutcher ropes off'n yer legs, blackie, an if'n y'run I'm a'gonna shoot yer legs fulla holes." He leaned closer, "Y'got that?"

The gag was still on, so Josh shook his head and said a small prayer. *Lord, if you feel like helping me, now's the time.* The man held Josh's arm as he stood, and then severed the rope holding his hands together. After regaining his balance, Josh was handed a shovel. Both men stood far enough away that Josh knew it was useless to attempt hitting one with the shovel and trying to tackle the other.

He went where the one pointed and started digging. They had another bottle of tequila open and were both laughing. The mean one said, "Betcha never thou'cha'd be a'diggin yer own grave hole, didja niggah boy? Haw, haw, he, he. Shoulda stayed home suckin yer black mammy's titty, stead o' gittin in with 'em lousy damn Rangers."

Josh's mind was racing as he dug. *Even drunk, that one'll put a bullet in me as soon as I run, but I guess it's…* he instinctually ducked when the man nearest him screamed. Thawack! He heard the same dull thud that came a split-moment before the scream, and now the second man was groaning as his hands grasped a shaft protruding from his chest. The first man was still on his feet and wobbling back and forth, but before Josh could do a thing, two more arrows hit each of his captors.

In the moon's glow he could see that they were both on the ground, groaning. The two men stiffened and then quivered and lay still.

Two braves from the Apache village, where he'd recently spent time resting, stepped from the darkness. One spoke, *"We wait until both in best place to shoot arrow."*

"Thank you, my friends, but how could you know where I was?"

"Bekkatee have vision when you leave. Chief say find you."

"I must have left you a good trail?"

"All white men leave trail like horse."

"How about black man?" Josh's grin was weak.

"We find you." The young Apache's face opened into a wide grin.

"Yes! If you do not, then I would be in that hole I was digging. Thank you for keeping your eyes to my trail. Josh turned toward the two men. *I guess we can use the hole for them?"*

Rick Magers

"*Better to leave for jaguar and he no look for us.*" The shorter of the two braves smiled. "*He always eat white meat but maybe like black people too.*"

"*Ho, ho, yes,*" the other added, "*we must bring you back alive so Bekkatee happy. Two white men dead, so jaguar happy too…good for everyone.*"

"*Except for those two.*" Josh nodded at the two men whose blood was draining into the sand.

"*Maybe good for them too. They not good in this life but maybe good in next one?*"

• • •

Joshua Harding sat across from Colonel Banenfield. "All these years, Joshua and we never sat down together, so I didn't even know if you like a drink of whiskey now n' then or not."

"Nossir, tried it once when I was with the cavalry but didn't like the feeling of not being in control. Never drank the stuff again. We never seemed to have time to get together, sir, but we sure made a lotta bad men pay the penalty for their crimes."

"We hell, Joshua, that was all you. As you sent 'em in, I filled out the paperwork and put the bastards in prison or in the ground." The colonel leaned forward. "Joshua, please send me a message when you plan to marry the lady and I'll be there. The Tonto are a good people, so you should have a good life with them. I met Wampanahah years ago; right after his daddy died and he became chief. He never said anything about even knowing there was a ranger station near his village."

The colonel poured himself another glass of whiskey, "His daddy was that way too. Minded his own business but was always ready to help keep the riff raff outa the area."

Joshua said, "His daddy was an African slave that was on a boat that sank, and he almost drowned. Made his way from the coast all the way here when he was just a boy."

"I always figured Wampanahah was half Negro, but he never told me anything about his daddy."

"Ain't told me much either," Josh commented, "but Bekkatee has told me all about her daddy." Josh chuckled quietly, "And everyone else in the village." He smiled wide, "She's very proud of her people."

Rick Magers

"She should be; they've stayed out of all the conflicts and went about their own way, living peacefully with everyone." The colonel thought a moment before continuing, "More like 'em and this country around here would be a pretty darn peaceful area to live in."

• • •

When Bekkatee and Joshua were wed, the colonel was standing nearby. Later that night he sat with them at the huge fire and listened as the medicine man told stories about the birth of his chief's daughter and her journey to womanhood.

The colonel came to them after the fire had burned low and most of the people had left for their sleeping skins. "Joshua, Bekkatee…I must get back to town, so I'll be fresh to meet the stage tomorrow, and greet some men who are gonna invest in the town. My horse has been waiting for me to unload som'n I brought for you two to get started off right. I'll be right back."

They waited and looked questioningly at each other. When he returned moments later, his saddlebags were draped over his shoulder.

"These're spare saddlebags that a fella left when he had old man Sandoval make him new ones, so you can keep 'em. There's fifty, ten-dollar gold pieces in 'em." He grinned, "Been puttin' a few aside for you right along. You never had no kinda life out there on the prairie, and you was born into slavery, so maybe this'll help you two get a good start."

When Chief Wampanahah died, ten years later, the council unanimously voted Joshua in as the new chief. The entire five hundred dollars, a very significant sum in those days, was spent making the village a better place for all to live.

Joshua never had to track down the killers of the colonel. He retired from the Texas Rangers at age seventy-five and remained in the area until his death at eighty-six. He often visited Joshua and Bekkatee, and was pleased when they named their first of three sons, after him.

Joseph Atahanna Harding would become chief when his father stepped down on his seventieth birthday, saying, "I have grandchildren to teach many things, and a wonderful wife who wants me to spend more time walking with her through her favorite meadow."

Joshua Harding's journey from a slave named Issana Donodado to the head of a tribe of Kawevikopaya Yavapai was at times difficult, but never dull. His life is still talked about when members of the Tonto Apache meet annually at places across the American west.

THE END

Rick Magers

5

TROUBLE in SUNDANCE

Abner Preston leaned against the roof post and listened to the little man that had just ridden into town to warn him. "That's right Sheriff, they said they was gonna stop in the first town they come to in Wyoming, and make 'em pay for what happened to young Billy."

The steel gray, unsmiling eyes looked so deeply into the little man's eyes that his mouth began to twitch. When the sheriff finally spoke, it was with the same deep Texas drawl that the little man had heard at his parole hearing earlier in the year. 'Gentlemen, I've come all the way from Wyoming to tell you I believe Homer Yarrow will walk the straight road now if you let him out.' This respected lawman's words had made the difference, and Homer was now free after ten years in prison.

"Got any idea what they're talkin' about, and who this Billy might be?"

"Nossir, all the years I rode with 'em I never know'd what they was talkin' about, half the time." He tried to smile, but those steel gray eyes refused to allow it, and the twitch returned as he added, "And I don't think they did either."

"Where'd you run into 'em, Homer?"

"Over in Spearfish, South Dakota. They was drinkin' and raisin' hell when I rode into town. I thought they was still down in Texas, so I got real curious 'bout what they was up to. They asked me if I wanted to ride this way with 'em, but I said I had a big job a'waitin' on me. I know'd from my parole hearing that you was up here, so I hightailed it here to letcha know." The mouth was twitching so bad now he had a hard time finishing the sentence, but he continued anyway. "They're goin' over to Deadwood and get a couple more guys before they head up this way."

Abner knew the little man was as nervous as a mouse in a cathouse, so he thanked him for the information, and told him to head on down the trail. He silently watched as he mounted up, but before riding on out of town Abner said, "You did good Homer; not gettin' in again with that bunch. Go on out west and find something that'll keep you outa the pen."

Sheriff Abner Preston didn't move quickly on anything, and it fooled a lot of men into thinking he was slow witted. It fooled more than a couple of them to death, and many more into long prison terms. He was still leaning against the post as he watched the little man ride west out of Sundance Wyoming. He had hardly moved a muscle, but his mind was now racing through the many options he had, to be able to prepare his town for the trouble heading their way.

Trouble heading his way was nothing new to the six and a half foot tall Texan, who appeared to be chiseled from granite. At fifty, the full head of hair now matched his gray eyes, and gave him the appearance of a much older man. Actually he was much older—thirty years as a Texas Ranger had given him two for one. He was every bit of a hundred when he accepted the job as Sheriff of Sundance, Wyoming—at least he felt he was.

Abner stayed away from publicity like a cat stays away from water, but lawmen have a way of keeping up with each other. When Wyatt decided to retire as Sheriff of Sundance he asked for a meeting with the city fathers. "Gentlemen, I know a good Texas Ranger who's retiring, but he's still got ten good years left in him. He's the man that cut off that gang heading for Mexico a coupla years back. The ones he and his men didn't kill were sent to prison for a long, long time. Abner Preston's his name, and he doesn't play around with these bums. He takes upholding the law very serious. If you'd like, I'll get in touch with him and see if he'll come up here in the mountains and take the job?"

Abner accepted the job, and soon found the nearly mile high town a refreshing change from the flat, sandy lands along the border of Texas. His first year in the mountain town of northeast Wyoming was exactly what he had expected it to be—boring. He was taking over from a great lawman, and knew it would be a town where law-abiding citizens expected to be able to walk their streets in safety. He planned to see to it that it stayed that way.

This month's great battle had been with a drunken young 'wannabe' in one of the local saloons. "Sheriff come quick, there's gonna be a shootin' over at The Sundance Saloon." Milford Pillrod, the town barber, rushed up to him in the early evening hours as he made his rounds through the rowdier section of town. He paused at the window of the gin mill to see what the situation was. When he entered and stood motionless, surveying the interior, he was an imposing figure. Much to the towns delight he still carried his twin, ivory handled, Colt 44's—butts forward. He wore a hand hammered, felt Stetson that would swallow most men's head. All eyes were on him as he allowed his eyes to adjust to the inside lighting. He stood silent a moment as he mentally recorded everything, and then strode quickly to the young man holding the gun while he stared blearily at the bartender, uttering slurred words that only his drunken young mind understood.

By the time the drunken fool realized something in his world was changing, it was too late to do anything about it. A hand that could grab a Texas Rattler about to strike—struck. The gun barrel was now pointing at the ceiling, as the ex-Ranger's other hand closed around the unfortunate young man's neck. He suddenly found himself dangling above the floor as his recent captives began laughing.

Sheriff Preston removed the pistol from the boy's hand and stuck it into his own belt, then without uttering a word, he grasp the desperado by the seat of his pants and walked out as the young man flailed his legs and arms.

When Homer disappeared into the afternoon sun, Abner turned and walked back into his office. "Might have a situation here a little different than we're use to, Brody." His deputy watched as the Sheriff talked to the man that had ridden up, but knew his boss well enough to keep his mouth shut and wait.

Rick Magers

"Got a gang headin' this way that I've dealt with before, down in Texas. They don't know I'm up here, and when they see me, they're gonna be mad as a hornet's nest that some fool like that kid in the saloon tonight had used for target practice."

"When you reckon they'll be gettin' here, Sheriff?" The young deputy watched as Sheriff Preston walked to the window and looked down the road. The Sheriff still had his Stetson on, and shoved it to the back of his huge head. The deputy glanced from it to the pearl handles of the revolvers, then down to the hand-tooled boots. Brody felt very lucky to be starting his career with this legendary lawman and thought, *there stands a lawman's lawman.*

After weighing the information that Homer had just passed on to him, he turned to the young Deputy he was beginning to like and trust very much. "Not less than three days; maybe as much as a week." He turned, went to his desk, and pulled out six silver badges. "You know who to give these to, Brody. Deputize 'em again, and tell 'em to keep in touch after Wednesday." He went to the gun rack as the Deputy headed for the door, then turned, "Tell 'em to come and check out their weapons as soon as they can. Locate our regulars, Brody, and tell 'em to stop by here to get briefed on the situation."

When the two regular peace officers were both in his office, the Sheriff explained about the potential danger headed their way. "You both know which part of town they'll naturally go to, so quietly go to each business and alert 'em. Tell each one we'll have everything covered, but as soon as they see this gang, or we let 'em know they're here, to lock up and keep out of sight till it's all under control."

Shortly after the two officers exited the office, five men and one six-foot-tall, stoutly built woman entered. They each had their temporary deputy badges concealed, so no one would be unnecessarily alarmed this early. He thanked each for arriving so promptly then said, "I've sent a message ahead, and if they can spare some men we'll be ready for anything, but just in case the message doesn't get through, let's be as ready as we can." He turned and handed each a shotgun, and a box of shells…double-ought buck. "It'll be dark as soon as we have coffee, then you can use one of those blankets to cover the guns with as you leave." He went to the huge pot and offered each a cup of the thick, black, Texas Ranger style coffee that would keep him on his feet for days. Three accepted; three politely refused. Each had experienced heartburn like never before after a cup of the Sheriff's coffee, but as always…three were a little tougher.

Twenty minutes later, Marilyn Bloodworth set her cup down and said in her no nonsense way, "It's dark enough that no one's gonna know what we have under these blankets, and I got things to do, so let's go."

Before he opened the door, Abner said, "This is as tough a gang as I know of, so let's be ready and careful."

On the fourth morning after Homer warned him, the Sheriff went to each business in the seedy section of town, and spoke to every owner. Even those that didn't like the man had come to respect him and his judgment—especially his uncanny intuitions. They listened when he said; "Be extra alert tonight, 'cause I got a feelin' they're on their way."

Marilyn Bloodworth stood behind the bar and watched as Sheriff Abner Preston came through the swinging doors of The Sundance Saloon. As always he stepped to the side to allow his eyes to get accustomed to the light. She watched thinking, *Damn! I'd love to get that big Texan between my sheets for a couple of hours.*

"Shot o' bourbon, Abner?" She smiled when he stopped in front of her.

"Sure," he grinned, and she felt something jump around in her stomach. "I got a feelin' about tonight…everyone ready?"

"Yep! I just talked to 'em all m'self."

He tossed the bourbon down and headed for the swinging doors, "Thanks darlin', I'll be around."

She couldn't take her eyes from his rear end as he walked back toward the bat-wing doors.

An hour after sundown he received a message from the officer that he'd stationed at the edge of town, toward the South Dakota border—they were riding into town.

He passed the message on, and was pleased at how quickly the business lights were turned off. All but The Sundance Saloon. He had pre-arranged with Marilyn to keep the place going full tilt.

He stood in the shadows across from her saloon and counted the gang members as they pulled up in front. *Thirteen…unlucky number*, he thought, *for them*. He remained motionless as they swung their legs over their mounts. His eyesight was still perfect, so in the saloon porch lights he had no trouble reading the letters on the back of their black leather jackets.

Rick Magers

NEW MILLENNIUM—HELL'S ANGELS
2007

THE END

Rick Magers

6

MYSTERIOUS GRINGO

Caleb Steelbender was contemplating his future as he moved slowly south into the depths of Mexico. *What a life we'll have if we get away with this. Pamela and me will live like royalty in France. Paris! Gay Pairee! Ahhhhh! If it's only half as pretty as the pictures, it'll be a great place to finish out my years.*

1922 Mexico was a good place to be if you liked Spanish people and spoke enough of their language to get the things necessary for good living. Alvaro Obregon had created a stable government that was moving rapidly ahead with economic and civil reform. General Antonio Lopez de Santa Anna had not yet become a prominent figure in Mexico's future.

When the gray haired old man arrived in San Neguaro driving a buckboard pulled by two big beautiful horses, he was viewed with more curiosity than most. Foreigners were not unknown to the five hundred residents of the town lying in the fertile valley south of Mt. Esqueloz. Over the years several had visited, but never any as huge as this man.

Jorge Gonzalez peered from beneath the shade of his sombrero as he leaned back against the adobe wall of Rosellito's Cantina. Beside him Pablo Molina appeared to be dozing, but Jorge knew he too was watching as the stranger stepped from the buckboard and rubbed his rear end.

"Buenos dias," the stranger said as he stopped in front of the two men. When no sound came from beneath the two umbrella size sombreros he leaned down to look directly into Jorge's black, curious eyes almost obscured by bushy black eyebrows. In passable Spanish he said, "My name is Caleb Steelbender, what are you called?"

When Jorge looked at the stranger's face, all he could see was the eyes. All other features faded away when the one lagoon blue eye and the other pure white one blinked once then held Jorge's almost hypnotically. When Caleb saw the startled look on the man's face he smiled wide exposing a mouthful of teeth that matched one eye perfectly. He was many years used to the same reaction when people first saw what he referred to as 'my pretty little white agate.' "Extrano, eh?," he said as he continued looking directly into Jorge's black eyes; now somewhat alarmed.

A little disarmed by the friendly smile, Jorge replied quietly, "Is it the eye of a devil?"

The smile widened, "Mama said yes, but no señor, it is a stone."

"Were you born with the stone?"

"No, but if we become friends I will tell you how I come to have a stone eye."

"You are going to be here awhile?" Jorge was still leery of this strange gringo but he was always on the lookout for a little cash and now sensed that some might be available.

"Yes, I want to buy land to grow food and flowers so I can live in this beautiful town of peace and beauty." Even though Caleb still struggled with the Spanish language he did well enough that both Mexican men understood him.

Pablo now spoke for the first time since Caleb arrived. Without moving his head he said, "How much land?"

Caleb turned toward the voice coming from the dark face barely visible beneath the sombrero, "How much do you have to sell me?"

"Not one handful but I know who has good land to sell."

The smile on Caleb's face was replaced by an intense stare as he moved his one functioning eye from one man to the other. "How can I do business with men whose names I do not know?"

Jorge spoke quickly to regain control over his friend who was about to take charge of a situation that might yield some profit. He gave Caleb his name, and then after saying, "I am the man to show you where to buy the land," he introduced Pablo.

"That is true if you wish to grow rocks," Pablo said considerably louder than he had spoken before.

"The land this bandit will take you to will not even grow cactus," Jorge said loudly.

"Well," Caleb said with a smile as he stepped back, "while you two argue I am going into this cantina for cool beer and warm tequila." At the swinging batwing doors he turned to add, "which I will be happy to share with my two new friends." Before the doors swung closed, the two men had joined him.

After a large clay mug of cool beer and two small tequilas each, Caleb asked, "Where can I leave my three large trunks so they will be safe until I decide where I will live?"

Jorge spoke first, "You are the only gringo here so you can leave them anywhere."

"Then may I ask where I can have my horses attended to?"

"Come," Pablo replied, "we will ride with you to the livery that is behind the hotel where you will stay."

The following morning Caleb met the two men at the same cantina that was also the only place that sold prepared food. By nightfall he had purchased five acres of land that was as nearly perfect for his needs as he could have hoped. He gave the two men the equivalent of a month's pay in their area, then headed toward his land as the sun began the evening journey toward its western resting place.

• • •

Six months later Caleb was sitting on the porch of his small, but comfortable adobe house watching the October sun drop below the mountains in the west. Jorge sat in the other handmade chair that Pablo arranged to have made for the man many were now calling the mysterious gringo. Pablo looked up from his perch against one of three posts supporting the porch roof. "Will you want me to arrange for the workmen to build the small building for your wagon?"

Before Caleb could answer, Jorge said loudly, "If he wants it built then I will arrange for it just as I have everything else."

Rick Magers

"Amigos," Caleb said quietly, "you have arranged for all I want done for now. I will build the small building myself."

Caleb worked diligently with the materials he arranged to be brought to his new home by Jorge and Pablo before sending them on their way. He soon had a small wooden building large enough to store his buckboard, tack, and the various tools he had either brought with him or purchased after arriving. The three large trunks were also stored against the rear wall.

Caleb's homestead was twelve miles from town, which prevented people from casually dropping in. He had things to do so he'd planned it that way. Caleb made it clear to Jorge and Pablo that he was interested only in property a good distance from town and other home sites. His days were spent behind one of his horses as it pulled the plow he bought from Pablo. "I will sell it to you much cheaper than a new one and it is better than a new one because I have broke it in to the ground it must work."

"But look how thin the plow blades are," Caleb said after riding with the elderly Mexican in the buckboard the twenty miles to his tiny stone house.

"Yes, that is true," Pablo replied, "and that is why it will easily cut into the earth." He tilted his head back to peer from beneath his drooping sombrero. He shook both gnarled hands in front of him as he said, "Thick blades are not for the land you have Señor Steelbender."

Caleb spent two hours each evening after supper working quietly inside the storage building with the door securely latched. When the wheelbarrow was filled, he opened the door and pushed the load of dirt into the field. After returning to the shed he latched the door and began digging in the trench again. After several trips he was satisfied that the trench was deep enough.

He covered the hole with boards and then sprinkled dirt over them. He opened the two doors on the end, which allowed him to push the buckboard in. Caleb stood back and looked carefully. Satisfied that the hole beneath the buckboard was not noticeable he closed the doors and placed the huge padlock through the latch on the inside. A similar padlock was placed on the outside of the small entrance door before heading to the house several yards away.

Rick Magers

Once inside the house, Caleb checked to be certain that the heavy curtain was in place over the one small window. He then dumped the contents of the bag he had removed from one of the trunks onto his single table. With the kerosene lamp pulled close, he spent two hours at the table without getting up.

Each night when the moon was dark he removed bags from the trunks to inspect them in the dim glow of the lamp. Two hours of fondling the items then he returned them to the bags. With them tucked into the waistband of his trousers Caleb moved swiftly through the darkness to unlock the shed door. The door was secured and he crawled beneath the wagon to remove two of the boards. He placed the bags, now wrapped in oilcloth beside the others and slid the boards back in place. Once the soil was spread back over the boards he held the oil lantern close to inspect the area. Satisfied that accidental eyes would see nothing unusual he returned to the house.

Shortly after the New Year began he had completed his task. The boards were removed and the hole beneath the buckboard was filled. Under cover of darkness he had brought wheelbarrow loads of dirt from his field. Careful tamping of the earth as he filled the shallow hole prevented all but a little settling. Each night he continuously added small amounts of soil to mask the settling until there was no evidence of a hole.

Caleb spent his mornings clearing a patch of land of rocks so the plow would last, then hitched one of the horses to it and worked the soil until he knew it was ready to plant in spring. To prying eyes that always seem to be where they're unwanted, Caleb appeared to be just another old American cowboy spending his late-in-life years preparing to grow flowers and vegetables. All had by now heard about his love for his mother and her love of the flowers that he was going to grow.

Every evening was the same. He prepared his meal then lay on the thin mattress and thought about his future. *Paris! I'll live a wealthy gentleman's life in Paris. Ahhhh!* Caleb's dreams were always the same—very pleasant.

As the mild winter gave way to spring, Caleb was anxious to begin planting the flower seeds his father brought from Spain many years earlier. His mother had always wanted to plant them in a field but had to settle for a pot on the balcony of her tiny New Orleans apartment. He carried the seeds since the day he made her a promise as she lay dying. "I will get a large piece of land mama and plant the whole thing with your flowers so you can see them from heaven."

• • •

Caleb's years had slipped quickly by and at forty he still had the seeds but was no closer to getting some land to grow them on. But then he met Pamela Daley. Julius Bront was Caleb's contact. Caleb brought him the items he removed from homes throughout the better sections of Texas. Caleb's father had used the old man for many years and always claimed, "Julius is the only honest front man I ever dealt with."

Caleb entered the small Dallas pastry shop and took a seat at the tiny table in the rear. Julius brought the coffee he knew his old friend's son would order. They were alone but from habit each spoke barely above a whisper. "Thanks for coming Caleb.
"You known her a long time?"
"Since her daddy brought her here from London." Julius glanced over his shoulder from habit, "He worked with me until that damn Doberman gave him a heart attack." Another furtive glance at his still empty shop; "She can be trusted."
That was good enough for Caleb. He sipped his coffee and waited. Moments later a woman entered that caused him to stop his cup half way to his lips. Good lord, he thought, *that is one gorgeous lady.*
He watched as the thirtyish, very trim woman walked directly to Julius. *That's a no bull shit gal*, Caleb thought as he sipped his coffee and watched her over the top of the cup. He sat his cup down when they came toward him.
"Caleb," Julius said, nodding at the woman beside him, "Pamela Daley, Toad's daughter." He turned and went back behind the counter to prepare for customers.
She pulled out one of the small wrought iron chairs and sat; all without taking her eyes from him. Caleb held her stare and waited until she finally spoke. "Julius says your dad was a great house man,

and that you're better." She pulled a pack of Peter Stuyvesant cigarettes from her jacket pocket without moving her eyes or blinking.

Caleb watched as she lifted a gold lighter to the cigarette and fired it up while her gunmetal gray eyes were still locked on his. He leaned toward her and locked his on hers. "My work speaks for itself. In twenty years I've never been caught." He paused as she lit a cigarette then said, "I don't hang around here too long; what's on your mind?"

"Have you heard of the VanDerGroot family?" She turned the tip of Peter a glowing red as she watched Caleb through smoke.

"Yeah! They invented rich. My dad always spoke of that house as if it was where all the world's wealth was."

Pamela smiled for the first time since arriving. Wealth was her favorite word. "A very significant part of it is." When Caleb remained silently staring she added, "I've seen it."

A smile was now forming on Caleb's face. "And you want me to go in n' get it?"

"Are you really the best?"

• • •

When the soil felt warm enough, Caleb began planting. He planted a small garden of vegetables near the house then began sowing his precious seeds across the rest of his five acres. He used his homemade rake to scratch the seeds into the earth as he walked back and forth across the entire field.

That evening he sat looking out over it and imagined what the flowers would look like. He finally collapsed in his bed; too tired to even prepare food. Caleb spoke quietly to the ceiling. "Very soon mama, you will find your beautiful flowers here and everywhere." He lay silently staring into the darkness, one eye unaware—one searching for the window and the stars that peeked at him on clear nights. "And I have found the woman of my dreams and the wealth I have dreamed of all my life." He slept peacefully dreaming of the bright orange flowers that he recalled struggling to survive on the balcony porch.

When the flowers began blooming, word spread. People began riding from town on mules and horses, and in carts pulled by donkeys. The people had never seen any flowers like them. "They are so bright," many commented. "What are they?" Others asked. Caleb did not enjoy having so many people around his homestead, but he was pleasant and obliging. "My father brought them from Spain," he answered, "and he called them Tears of the Sun." He smiled at a small wagon with three old ladies sitting with smiles on their wind worn faces and said, "I will give anyone who will plant them some seeds when they are ready."

As the beautiful orange flowers bloomed on sturdy stalks from one end of Caleb's five acres to the other, Jorge supervised the two young boys he had hired to cut off the seed filled buds each day that had dried after blooming. A third young boy was brought to go from budplucker (as Caleb called the other boys) to budplucker with a two wheel cart collecting the buds. "Dump them into these wire racks on the bottom," Jorge instructed the boy, "then shove them back beneath the glass panels."

Caleb and Jorge had worked together to build the seed drying racks. They were made of wooden boards with wire mesh bottoms to allow the seeds to drop onto a tray beneath as they dried. They were all under glass panels that Jorge arranged to be built by a window maker. The panels were on the south end of the house so the sun would be on the seeds beneath all day. "This is a marvelous invention you have created Caleb," Jorge said after seeing it in operation.
"I can't take credit for inventing it Jorge," Caleb replied, "they have been using similar ones in the old country for many years."
"But you said you have made it better."
"Yes, I think I have by using these glass panels to dry them faster so our boy can keep ahead of the seed pluckers."
Together the two men rotated the three tiers of seed trays so the one closest to the top was quickly drying the buds. They used a paddle to gently tap and roll the buds to release the seeds, which fell through the wire. When a tray was emptied of its seeds another was ready. The two seed pluckers, the young seed collector, Jorge, and Caleb did this work three days a week from July when the flowers bloomed until October when colder weather moved into their valley.

"There must be millions of seeds in those bags," Jorge said after the last rack was emptied. He looked at the stalks out in the field that still had many flowers on them, "You are sure they will come back every year?"

Rick Magers

Caleb lowered the leather water bag to hand it to Jorge as he swallowed, then answered. "My father told mother that when they got their land these flowers would re-seed themselves forever if a few buds were left on the stalks to dry."

"Maravilloso," Jorge said before taking another drink of the cool water.

"Yes it really is a marvelous flower. The buds left on soon dry then slowly droop down until they are pointing straight at the ground so the seeds will disperse for another crop the following year."

"And all we must do is lightly rake the earth after pulling up the stalks?"

"That's it, according to my father."

"And you will be back to see them blooming?"

"Sure will," Caleb said, "even getting these seeds to the people who will market them, plus my other business won't keep me from being here to see mama's flowers bloom."

"She will be very pleased when she looks down from heaven to see what you have done for her."

"Yes, I'm sure she will," Caleb answered, "because all she ever saw before was the few she could grow in her little balcony pot."

● ● ●

In early April Caleb had the two horses hooked to the buckboard. He had spent many nights of the long winter filling the seed packets he had ordered from San Antonio. He was very pleased with the finished product. *If I'm stopped for any reason,* He thought, *I'll look like a flower seed salesman bringing a rare beauty to this barren landscape.*

His precious bags of pearls, rubies, diamonds and emeralds that had once hung from the neck of the Russian Czar's wife were packed beneath the false bottom of each trunk. Six inches of seed packets covered the bottom and three trays of packets covered them. The trunks were loaded onto the flat area behind the seat of the buckboard where Caleb would handle the team. The trunks were then covered with oilskin tarps.

After Caleb settled himself on the seat, he looked down at Jorge. "You have become a good friend, Jorge, and I look forward to seeing you in the spring." *But only if you come to Paris,* he thought.

Rick Magers

"Do not worry about your house and building because I have sent out word that I am the caretaker in your absence."

When Caleb took hold of the reins and was about to release the brake with his foot Jorge said, "You never told me about your white agate and how you come to have it."

Caleb removed his foot from the brake and said, "You are right my friend. I have been busy and forgot. I was working at night doing a special job in a house for a wealthy family. Not being familiar with the house I stumbled in the poor lighting and fell. The end of the staircase had a wooden spike instead of a round ball and I landed on it with my eye." He grinned and waved with a finger from his eye out, "Pop! Out it went and that's been my dark side ever since."

"And the white agate? You made it yourself?"

"Ah ha," Caleb said and picked the reins back up. "You give me credit as a craftsman that I could never be. No my friend, A doctor sent me to a man who makes eyes for clumsy fools like me."

He slapped the horses and braced himself as they headed north along the narrow dirt road. By noon he had altered his course for Puerto Vallarta where Pamela would soon arrive on the ship that was to take them to Europe.

"Yes," the small old Mexican said quietly as he watched the buckboard leave, "we are friends, but you are certainly a mysterious gringo."

● ● ●

The trip to Puerto Vallarta was an uneventful three days. Caleb located a spot on both nights that concealed him from the few people passing by in wagons. Pamela's timing was correct and the sailing vessel arrived the following afternoon. Caleb paid the livery stable extra to allow him to stay near his horses. "I've had them since they were born and this is the first time they will ever be in a building other than their own stable back home." He was concocting a story about where he was from, but quickly realized that the man's only interest was the money. When he paid the old Mexican, he added a little extra and thanked him for understanding. *I ain't leaving these trunks for any reason.* He looked around then said quietly "I'll need a bucket to shit in."

Rick Magers

After finding an old stall bucket he placed it in the corner and got out some beef jerky, hard tack, and the huge jug of cold coffee he made before leaving. He brought fresh straw to make a bed then placed his 12-gauge shotgun nearby. Caleb knew his horses in the next stall would alert him if anyone came near, so after eating he lay back and dreamed of Pamela—riches…and the life of a gentleman.

Caleb followed Pamela's instructions, made during their last night together in New Orleans at the Hotel Bayou LeVoiux. "If those flowers are as good as you say then they'll be the perfect cover as you lay low in Mexico until the search for the burglar dies down." She continued talking as she moved to the table for another glass of gin, but Caleb had great difficulty concentrating on her words. Her voluptuous naked body flushed all but that from his mind. . . . . . "and leave the wagon and trunks at the livery. Whoever he is I doubt he'll even wonder where you went and will soon toss those seed packets and sell the trunks and everything."
She stood smiling at him. "I do believe everything I just said was wasted on your lusty mind, you dirty old man."
Caleb caressed her body with his eyes before speaking." You're right, but I also memorized everything the first time we discussed it."

In the darkness of the stall Caleb removed the jewels and placed them into the small suitcase Pamela had given him that same night. After the livery stable man left for the day he went directly to the dock and bought passage to Calais, France. He knew that he and Pamela would act as strangers during the voyage in case an insurance detective or someone from the police was following her. "Once we get to Calais," she said through smoke from Peter's burning head, "I can give anyone the slip and we'll rendezvous at the Hotel Rue Gaston."

Not a person on board would have guessed that the two people; one old man with an artificial eye and the beautiful woman with gunmetal-gray eyes had ever met, let alone been brief lovers. Nor would anyone have guessed that the handsome young Spaniard in the cabin next to hers was actually her lover of many years—and business associate.
The ship docked at Santander, Spain on the Bay of Biscay for two days. When darkness fell across the decks on the last night in Spain,

Pamela slipped very silently toward Caleb's stateroom. She paused to look at Maarten who was standing in the shadows watching the deck in both directions. When he nodded she went to Caleb's door and knocked. When she told Caleb who it was he opened to allow her to slip quietly inside—and into his arms. "I can stand it not a moment longer, my darling Caleb," she spoke convincingly…he needed little convincing.

• • •

When the ship pulled away from the dock in Santander at dawn, Pamela, Maarten, and the suitcase full of jewels were all on a train heading toward Milano, Italy. The Spaniard said a second time, "I still think you should have killed the old fool."

Pamela loved the sexually dynamic young Spaniard but she knew he was a fool. "Marty my love, do not let your jealousy cloud you're good sense." She leaned over and kissed him. "I pretended each time that it was you inside me. We are thieves but not killers, my darling."

The ship was far at sea when Caleb began recovering from the large dose of sedative Pamela put in the bottle of his favorite champagne. When he attempted to rise, a terrible pain went through his head. Thinking it was still night he called, "Pamela." After several more calls to her he reached up and pulled the string to his bedlamp. Nothing. He pulled it several times but still no light.

"Come quickly sir," the young cabin attendant said to the ship's officer, "there is a blind man who has been stabbed in the eyes."

• • •

"And besides," Pamela said, "how will a blind man be of any use to the police. They'll just listen to his story and think him insane."

Maarten shook his head and the dark wavy hair moving so effortlessly excited Pamela. "He probably will be insane very soon."

Pamela sat silently in the office in Milano, Italy as Maarten opened the suitcase to display the jewels to the mob boss who had fronted a small fortune to pull off the biggest jewel heist of the century. He looked impassively at the contents then nodded for his jeweler to come and inspect them.

• • •

A short time after the VanDerGroot family returned from a lengthy Asian holiday, Pamela informed them that she was returning to London. The theft of the jewels was discovered soon after she was gone.

    Emil VanDerGroot turned to his wife Hildeguarde, "It's difficult to believe that anyone, even a domestic like that English woman, could believe that people such as us would ever have the real jewels just locked in the safe in a house."
    A scowl crossed Hildeguarde's face as she said, "Even those paste copies I wear at functions cost us more than that woman will earn in her lifetime, so I hope the insurance detective catches her and whoever helped her.

• • •

They never did. Julius Bront's body was found beaten and cooking in one of his huge pastry ovens. Caleb died in an asylum for the insane soon after reaching the next port. Parts of Pamela and Maarten were found all over Italy but were never identified. No one actually ever tried to identify them.

    The flowers still bloom all over Mexico every year. Many people call them Mexican Sunflowers but some of the old people still refer to them as Tears of the Sun.

THE END

Rick Magers

7

HIGHPOCKETS DANDY

The stage pulled into Two Stores. When it finally came to a stop, a cloud of dust surrounded the trail-worn old stagecoach. The driver tied off the reins before standing to stretch. This was the third stagecoach he'd worn out for the Madeline Henley Stage Line. The young man riding shotgun opened the old double-barreled 10 gauge shotgun and removed both shells, then placed the weapon beneath the seat.

Julep Brent stretched as he watched his new guard. The boy gripped the rail beside his seat, and in one lithe movement was sailing from the driving area. He let go and landed smoothly beside the coach and removed his new leather hat. He used the hat to brush away dust that had covered his clothes on the ride from San Diego to Two Stores. Replacing the hat atop his head of curly red hair, he opened the stagecoach door.

"Watch your step, ma'am." He held Madeline's hand as though she was fragile and might break if she fell.

Little chance of that happening, because Maddy, as she preferred, was one of the few madams with sense enough to close her Los Angeles brothel to begin a new life and enjoy the fortune she had accumulated. Her marriage to Rudolf Henley was the icing on an already well-baked cake. He was the attorney who led the small coastal city of Los Angeles into the nineteenth century.

Rick Magers

The death of Rudolf left Madeline very sad, because they had enjoyed a good relationship from her early days as Los Angeles' premier rest and relaxation spot for the many weary, rich and famous travelers.

When Madeline Bloodworth's parents perished in the fire that left their Australian three-story home a mere pile of ashes, she returned from visiting her aunt in Queensland, to find herself alone on a twenty thousand acre cattle station in New South Wales. She was a gorgeous young twenty-year-old who hated the barren continent the day she arrived with her parents from London. Madeline was then a vivacious fun seeking ten-year-old, and now at twenty, she still hated the country…especially ranch life…'if you can call it a life' Madeline repeatedly told her friends in letters sent home to London.

The station sold quickly to a neighboring cattle rancher and Madeline was soon aboard a clipper ship heading toward a new future in California.

Rudolf Henley had recently lost his wife to cancer and decided to put the memory behind him by moving to North America. Originally an astute businessman in England, he smiled when the beautiful young blonde responded to his suggestion that they save money by sharing a cabin aboard the clipper. You're a handsome man for your age and I've enjoyed dining with you as we've waited for the ship to be ready for us to board, but Rudy, I don't do anything just for the fun of it. She smiled coyly and raised her glass of champagne.

He loved women with spunk who always kept their financial betterment at the forefront of their lifestyle. He joined her with his raised glass. "I'll see to it that your passage money is returned and that all of your belongings are transferred to my, excuse me, our cabin. When we dock in Los Angeles I will finance you in the establishment of any new business venture that you choose, because it will most certainly be a success and make us both wealthier."

By the time Madeline Bloodworth's twenty-fifth birthday arrived, her brothel, The Seaside Palace, was famous from one end of the west coast to the other. Wealthy businessmen and temporally rich gold miners made visits so frequently from distant points that she created Seaside Travel Coach. It was a public stagecoach line, but special customers were given a pass to ride free to her brothel from any place it stopped.

Rudolf spent many nights in Madeline's arms and knew that he was one of very few to ever enjoy that privilege. He always arrived with a gift of pearls, diamonds, and hand crafted gold jewelry, and always left a pile of money when he departed.

On his sixtieth birthday he retired from the board as CEO of his giant conglomerate, Henley Industries, Pty Ltd. At a private birthday party that same evening in the main ballroom of The Seaside Palace, he stood among the few close friends who had been invited. Tapping his crystal champagne glass with a fork, he quieted the crowd. "All of you know that Madeline and I have been both business partners and close friends for many years. It is with extreme pleasure to announce that to my very simple question to her several months ago; will you please marry me? Madeline Bloodworth answered, yes."

He turned toward the spiral staircase and pointed to the top. "You all know that we both do everything our own way, so it shouldn't surprise anyone to learn that we'll be wed tonight amongst this gathering of our friends."

When Madeline, who was waiting behind the door, heard Rudolf announce, "And now I give you the future Mrs. Madeline Henley," she nodded to the seven-foot-tall Caribbean Negro from the island of Trinidad, who had been her bodyguard and personal valet for many years.

The 300 pound black mountain opened the door and stepped aside as she walked to the stairs. When forty-year-old Madeline stood momentarily on the top step, the crowd below gasped then began applauding thunderously.

Weighted down by custom-made apparel, she moved slowly downward. Her right hand was on the cherrywood banister rail and Ishmael Osanna held the other. Her gown was created in Paris by Antoine Pillar and had sixty pounds of gold filigree blended magnificently with imported Chinese golden colored silk. It took, however, several moments for the eyes below to notice the wedding gown. The tiara resting on her golden hair was made of solid gold with seventy diamonds leading the way to a huge diamond in the center...all eyes were at first locked onto it.

When the crowd's eyes left the tiara they rested momentarily on a necklace made of 300 perfectly matched pearls. The gown sparkled as she descended the stairway, and then they saw her shoes. Woven from golden strands by Rome's most famous master shoemaker, Guiseppe Guido, each had 200 small diamonds attached.

• • •

The marriage was a good one that lasted ten years, and ended only when Rudolph died. Madeline had already sold the brothel a few years earlier and it was changed to a plush hotel that catered to the very wealthy. Many of the same customers continued to frequent the place but all missed the elegant proprietor and her many lovely young women imported from all areas of the world. Many older men sat in the opulent lobby with closed eyes—dreaming of days past.

Madeline renamed the coach service to the Madeline Henley Stage Line, and traveled on it often. Stock in her husband's company outgrew her ability to spend the money, so she embarked on a tour of philanthropy across California to give assistance to the needy in her adopted country. She left every town she visited with a new school, church, and medical facility along with funds to hire a preacher, doctors, and teachers. Her Los Angeles offices handled all necessary arrangements to ensure each town was sent funds as needed.

"Young man," she said to the shotgun guard, "I saw your leap from the seat and if you don't break something irreparable, I do believe you will become famous in a circus some day."

"No ma'am," the handsome youth responded with a smile, "I'm gonna be the world champion bronco rider some day. I'm workin' for this stagecoach line and savin' m'money to get the gear I need."

"Well, good luck on your venture. I'm going to get a room and stay here a few days, but right now I'm starving. Where's a good place to eat?"

"Well ma'am," the young man grinned again, this here town is still called Two Stores, but there's sure more'n that now. See that little store across the street there?" He pointed, "The one painted red."

"Yes!"

"It was the third store in Two Stores, folks say, and it's still here 'cause the food's hot, good, and reasonably priced."

Rick Magers

"Then that's where I'm heading, thank you." The huge black man had exited the stage while she was talking to the young red headed guard. "Hungry, Ishmael?"

"Yes'm! I could eat the saddle if the horse was already et."

"Let's go see what they have, and then I'll get us each a room in the hotel there." She turned back to the young guard who was helping another passenger from the stage. "Are the beds in the hotel good ones with real mattresses?"

"Don't really know ma'am, can't afford a room, so I sleep in the stagecoach."

Madeline looked up at the driver who was still rubbing his back and stretching. "Hey Julip, you still have a gal in every town?"

"Almost, but when I ain't I sleep with the team out in the livery. Wouldn't know nothin' about *sleeping*" he emphasized the word, "in them hotel beds."

The guard wrinkled his brow as he looked from his driver to the lady. He turned when the last passenger stepped to the ground and spoke. "I'm sure gonna find out ma'am, because I'm gonna try out whatever bed they have available."

The young guard watched as the man walked away. When the driver called, he turned. "Hey Tad, take this cash box." Julep hefted the small steel box over the side and lowered it down.

Tad took the safe and lowered it to the ground then turned toward the passenger again. He was wearing a trail-stained white shirt tucked into the waist of bright blue trousers. He was a man who advertised his right to enjoy good living. His large belt came together just below his breasts. White socks protruded from dusty brown shoes that covered feet three inches beneath the cuff of his pants. His blue jacket was held to his suitcase by the straps, and he carried it in one hand. With the other hand he fanned his sweating, nearly bald head with the brown derby he carried.

When Julep was standing beside him, Tad asked about the woman with the black. "Is that black giant her husband?"

"Nope! That's Madeline Henley and she owns this stage line. That big guy's her bodyguard, and he goes everywhere she goes." He spit tobacco juice into the dust at his feet, "Been with her since she came to Californy. Heard he kilt a few men what tried to do her harm."

The fat little man in highpocket trousers was still on the porch trying to catch his breath. Tad nodded with his chin, "Whacha reckon that fella with his pants pockets up under his armpits is doin' here?"

After another blast of tobacco juice, Julep answered. "My reckon is he's a drummer sellin' life insurance or som'n what don't take a lotta totin' from one town to the next."

Tad lifted his hat and dried his forehead on the sleeve of his shirt. "Sure wears funny clothes."

"Yeah, most of them fellers what sell stuff in towns along these trails dress up like peacock birds. Reckon they wanna kinda stand out so's we'll see 'em better. Most folks call 'em highpocket dandies. C'mon Tad, here comes McAdler and his Messikin t'git the stage n' take her back to the livery, so let's you n' me go git our free meal n' two free beers."

The two trail-weary men took their time and thoroughly enjoyed the steak and potato meal and two beers offered at each overnight stop.

Madeline had entered about the time the two men moved into the bar for their beers. She went to a small table near the wall and the black giant stood behind her leaning against the wall. His dark eyes roamed endlessly back and forth across every person in the hotel bar. The bartender knew who she was, so he came around from behind his workstation to get her order.

"Hello Mrs. Henley, I was tending bar at the Mustang Hotel in Amarillo when you visited last year. Would you like me to make you a brandy cocktail like you had there?"

"Why yes! That would be a great way to end a very dusty ride."

He went back behind the bar and ignored the demands of his customers. When Madeline's drink was made he returned to her table. Ishmael watched him closely but continued to scan the bar's patrons.

She stared at the older man a moment after he arrived with the tray holding her cocktail, then said, Orville, isn't it?

The man almost dropped the tray and his mouth fell open. "Good Lord, you remember my name?"

She smiled as he sat the drink in front of her. "I remember the name of every bartender who correctly prepared my favorite cocktail. I don't recall her name, but I remember a Mexican wife who brought her husband tortillas and chorizo, every day promptly at noon."

The man beamed when he said, "Esmeralda."

Rick Magers

"Treat her good, Orville; she's a greater treasure than you could possibly know."

Julep and Tad were at the close end of the bar and could hear the conversation. "Boy oh boy," Tad softly commented, "that lady sure has a good memory."

Julep smiled saying, "Sure does." He would never mention it but knew that Madeline probably had the names of a few hundred men etched into her memory. He had driven many of them to The Seaside Palace over the many years he had worked for her. He was at the reins of the first stagecoach when the company was still The Seaside Travel Coach.

A short time after going to work for her, he proved his worth as a valued member of Madeline's team by whipping up a hidden shotgun and killing a bandit bent on robbing her wealthy passengers. She awarded him with fifty, ten-dollar gold pieces and put a shotgun guard on every coach from that day forth. He thanked her for the coins but smiled and asked, "Now that I'm wealthy, kin I spend some time one night with one o' those beauties of yours?"

Madeline grinned back and then laughed hard. "Julep, tell ya what. Tell me your birthday and after you've been with me for five years, you can spend your entire birthday night with one of 'em every year as long as you're with me."

He looked forward to his birthday every year after the fifth one rolled around, and once commented to a friend who also drove a stagecoach, but for another company. "Madeline Henley is a good gal and I plan on workin' fer her till I can't climb up in the seat any more." He meant it and was saddened to hear that she was selling The Seaside Palace, but was pleased when she informed him that he would get to spend two days, with all expenses paid, each birthday at the hotel as long as he lived.

Julep and Tad, as well as most of the men at the bar, turned when they heard the loud voice of Curly Brown. Nobody noticed but Ishmael tensed, and relaxed muscles tightened when Curly screamed just beyond the batwing doors leading into the bar.

"Gitcher ass away from that goddamm door y'damn Messikin bastard an if y'come in the bar I'll put a bullet up yer greaser ass." The doors flew apart and Curly strutted in—all five feet of him.

Rick Magers

He staggered to the bar and slammed his tiny fist down. "Gitcher ass over here and pour me some whiskey, Orville."

After the portly bartender poured a double shot of rye for Curley, he turned to go back to his other customers. "Leave that goddamm bottle, you fat turd."

Curley was the only brother of hired killer, Latch McAllister. They rode in the previous year with their five-man gang and bought a ranch from the widow of a man mysteriously shot. He'd been heading to a small town a day's ride away to order supplies. Curley was told to remain with one other gang member and keep the ranch running so they would have a place to go when things got hot. The runt outlaw made a point of telling everyone in Two Stores that if they messed with him, his brother's gang would return and set things right.

Before the first glass of rye was settled in Curley's stomach, the batwing doors opened and in walked Highpockets. He was bathed, powdered, and dressed in his best. The pants were bright red with a white ruffled silk shirt tucked in. Red suspenders held the pants even higher than they were when he stepped from the coach. The same shoes had been polished and the white socks now created a five-inch border between his pant's cuff and the shoes. He naively walked to the bar and stood beside Curley. Raising his hand he yelled to Orville, "Please bring me a beer when you have time."

Curley looked in the mirror at the man beside him. Turning slowly with his glass of rye, he looked the man up and down then began laughing hysterically. Between gasps and laughter he asked, "What in the hell are you, a circus clown?" Nobody had yet heard the man's name, so Julep and Tad strained to hear when he addressed Curley. Holding out his hand he said, "Emerson Tidwell at your service, sir."

Curley just looked at the man's hand and laughed. "Ain't about to shake hands with anyone looking like you, 'cause whatever the hell you have might be catching." He pounded the bar with his child-like hand and laughed until tears ran down his face.

Julep and Tad were amazed by Highpocket's reply as he turned to his beer that Orville sat in front of him. "Might be a good idea because yours might be too, and I'm already short enough."

It took a moment for the slur to register in Curley's drunken brain. When it did, he wheeled toward Emerson and was reaching for his gun when a vise-like grip locked his hand before reaching the pistol at his side. A quiet but deadly voice spoke to him. "Missus Henley own dis hotel now mon, so ain gonna be no shootin in here." Ishmael reached around with his free hand and removed Curley's pistol. "You git dis back when you leave." The huge black man returned to his position against the wall. Curley's old pistol was shoved into Ishmael's belt beneath his long black coat. His own Colt lay butt forward in a custom holster on the other side.

Curley quickly poured himself another shot of rye, and after downing it he turned to Emerson and growled, "Be outa this town when I get here tomorrow you silly lookin' freak or I'll put a bullet right through this big buckle." Curley placed the end of his tiny right forefinger directly on Emerson's belt buckle, but failed to notice what was on it in silver letters. He added in a leering voice, "And that'll send it straight through your heart, you highpockets dandy."

Julep and Tad both noticed that Emerson didn't appear ruffled at all when he answered Curley. "Well sir, I have business here in Two Stores so I can't leave. If you're suggesting a duel, then I suppose the town should be notified so they can attend."

To Julep, Curley's grin appeared a bit forced. He knew Curley's brother had been killed during a bank robbery in Los Angeles and his gang had been caught. *I wonder if Curley'd be so brazen if he knew he was all alone now?* Curley tossed down the whiskey and threw a gold coin on the bar before turning back to Emerson. "Do whatever you wanna do, but at noon tomorrow I'll be comin' in from m'ranch, so either be gone or be ready to take a one way trip up to the bone orchard." He turned to glare at the huge black man who had his gun.

Ishmael walked through the batwing doors and on through the lobby to the front porch. Moments later Curley came out and snatched the gun that Ishmael was holding out. The six cartridges were in Ishmael's pocket as he turned and re-entered the hotel.

The following day, Emerson had his display set up in the large room behind the lobby that was used for weddings and such. Large posters of his merchandise lined the walls. A portable, folding tripod was on the table where he would give his presentation.

**ALL ORDERS MUST BE PAID IN FULL
AND WILL BE DELIVERED PROMPTLY**

Rick Magers

Emerson pulled the gold watch from his pocket. *Almost noon. I hope that little fella is still sleeping off the whiskey.* He turned the elaborately decorated timepiece over to read the inscription on the back. It had been given to him by the creator of the company that he worked for, and was his most treasured possession.

~ To Emerson Tidwell ~
A loyal representative of
this company's merchandise
and the best of the best
who use it.

He opened a leather case and removed the contents. After adjusting the belt he headed toward the front porch. It appeared to Emerson that every adult in town was lining the side of the road. *I hate it when things work out like this, but it will certainly bring potential customers to my presentation—always does,* he said to himself. He looked in the direction that the old stagecoach driver had told him that Curley would ride in from.

Moments later, he spotted two horses on the road. He walked to the center of the street and stood waiting.

Curley and his backup turned their mounts toward the small saloon and dismounted. After looping the reins around the rail a couple of times, they both headed toward the lone figure standing in the center of the dirt road.

Curley spoke quietly, "When I count to three, start shootin'."

"Well I'll be damned," Curley said quietly, "that highpockets dandy has a gun strapped on."

"Yeah," his man answered, "lookit how high the dern thing is."

The gap between the three men had closed enough and Curley began quietly counting.

"One . . . two . . . three."

Both men reached for their pistols.

Men would later swear that the fat man wearing his pants high on his belly had his gun out the entire time and only had to raise it. Other men told them, "You shoulda come to his salesman show."

Rick Magers

One hour later, Emerson opened the double doors and welcomed the huge crowd to his presentation—Julep and Tad were among them.

He began with an sincere apology. "Gentlemen, I truly regret the disgusting event that occurred in the street earlier. There will always be those men among us who threaten the safety of hard working citizens who want to live their lives in peace. When confronted by those men, as I was today, you can place your trust and your life in a Colt firearm. Each poster has the information about the weapon on it and the order number in the lower right hand corner along with the price delivered to you. I carry only one model and usually give a demonstration of its balance and accuracy, but unfortunately you have all seen that an hour ago. I will however demonstrate how easily a Colt can be drawn from our custom holster."

He opened the leather case again and strapped on the weapon. He opened the cylinder to show everyone that it was not loaded. Emerson drew the pistol several times before replacing it to the case.

When the stagecoach rumbled out of town a few hours later, there were still a few who said it was a trick of some kind. "Ain't no man alive what kin yank a pistol out'n a holster thet dern fast, and plug two fellers straight through the heart."

THE END

Rick Magers

8

BLACK WARRIOR

The young boy watched as his mother and father moved carefully but swiftly along the row of cotton. He was not yet five, which was the age children were sent into the Shriff Plantation fields to begin learning the tasks they would do all of their lives.

Earlier in the morning, Brutus had grabbed him by the arm when he followed his parents from their hovel. The sun wouldn't wash away the frightening darkness for another hour, so the boy was terrified when Brutus grabbed him. "This picaninny ain't no goddamn child." He lifted the boy off the ground and held him in the light of the lantern held by his assistant. "You keepin him at home when he's already old enough to work?" He glared at Lilly, the boy's mother.

Before the six-foot-tall, pretty Watutsi slave could answer, the boy's father, Joe Shriff spoke. "Nossuh, mistah Brutus. Master Shriff done got all de boy's papers up deah in de mansion, and he ain gwine be five till nex month come roun." The tall slender six-foot-ten-inch tall, muscular Watutsi held his homemade rag hat in his hands. "He still juss a boy, mistah Brutus, suh."

Brutus threw the boy to the ground and unfurled the rawhide whip so quickly that it was lashing Joe's back before the slave realized that he had overstepped a boundary by speaking without first asking permission. "When you have something to say nigger, wave your hat like all the rest." He turned to the terrified boy who was still lying on the ground. "What the hell's your name?" When the boy just stared, the plantation overseer turned to Lilly. "He deaf?"

"Nossuh mistah Brutus, he juss scared and he ain't got no name anyway, cause we juss calls him Boy"

"Git up off that ground, Boy." He leaned down and glared at the shivering child and motioned for him to rise. "That's better. Now git in there n' fetch yourself a hat and cotton bag, **Boy**," he emphasized the last word, "because it's time you started earning all of the food you're eatin."

The child was back so fast with a rag hat and bag that Brutus laughed. "You can damn sure fetch, boy. Haw, haw, haw, haw, that's your name from now on, boy; Fetch Shriff." He motioned toward the still-dark fields with the whip's handle, "Gitcher asses out in them fields and git ready to earn the food and shelter we give you niggers. If I see this pickaninny playing or slacking, I'll show him how this whip'll help him git a move on." That evening the boy's name was entered into the same Shriff Plantation log where the hogs, cattle, and other livestock were listed—Fetch Shriff.

Colonel Shriff summoned Brutus to the mansion. The British butler looked at the man's mud-covered boots but said nothing as he led him to the Colonel's office. After closing the door for him, Mister Anson pulled a satin cord. In less that a minute four cleaning girls arrived. He said nothing, but motioned toward the boot prints and then returned to the silver service he was cleaning.

"Good evening Brutus. Here's a glass of that new brandy you said you enjoyed when last you were here. I won't keep you away from your duties, but since I will be gone for a fortnight to Savannah, I wanted to let you know that I'll be leaving tomorrow morning, two days earlier than I had expected. I plan to inquire about rumors of rising cotton prices in Europe, and see if there will be slaves arriving anytime soon."

Brutus tossed the brandy down, and then assured the colonel that all would be fine during his absence, and returned to his duties. He glared at the snobby butler who turned away from the offensive odor. Once outside he thought of the men he must locate. *Jesus! Three bucks each night for missus Shriff for damn near two weeks; bet she'll want me in her bed again a coupla times too…damn.*

Joe was selected to service Adeline Shriff at least once each time the colonel left the plantation. Joe knew that his wife Lilly was forced to service Brutus when he was in the mood, and there was nothing that either of them could do about it. Each time she returned there were bite marks and cigar burns in disgusting areas of her once-lovely body. Each time, something deep inside Joe attempted to erupt but Lilly always calmed him. "Dat boy we's got gonna need a mama an a daddy, so don't do nuttin crazy. We gots to teach him bout de bess way to git along wit dese mean white folks." Her gaze drifted out toward the endless fields of cotton. "Mebbe we kin all escape some day an go back to Africa."

"Dat a sho nuff nice dream, darlin, but ain nevah gonna happen."

• • •

Brutus kept a list of the bucks that were to service Adeline Shriff. Each was told when to leave the fields, and to go directly back to work when she was finished with them. Most were happy to get a break from the brutal sun of the cotton fields, even if it meant climbing into bed with the plantation owner's sow.

Brutus always informed his ten assistants when 'Missus Pickle Barrel'…as they all referred to Adeline Shriff, would have bucks coming and going all day and night. He didn't want one to shoot a slave—thinking he was skulking around the mansion. One of Brutus' assistants once commented to a fellow assistant; "That dern bedroom light never goes out the whole time the Colonel's away, an by golly if she wasn't bigger'n this blamed hoss, I'd git in that dern line m'self."

His pal laughed, "Wouldn't bother me none atol about her bein so fat, but good God a'mighty, that woman's ugly." He shook his head and chuckled, "Betcha even them nigger bucks have a hard time keepin it up."

Mid way through the Colonel's trip, Brutus sent word with his number one assistant to bring Lilly Shriff to his log cabin, which sat a short distance from the mansion. It was a small but comfortable home for a bachelor, having a separate bedroom apart from the living room and kitchen. When he accepted the job on the Shriff Plantation; six hundred acres of cotton fields, a short distance northwest of Valdosta, over twenty years previously, Colonel Shriff allowed him to supervise a group of slaves to construct the dwelling. Brutus positioned it with winds favorable to keep the smell from the slave's tarpaper and stick shacks from disturbing his olfactory senses.

Joe looked up from his row of cotton as Hans Trundt, a German immigrant known as The Kaiser, stopped his huge black gelding and spoke to Lilly. "You! Schwartzer, grabbink dis rope; der boss vants you." She knew better than to even glance back at Joe, who was ahead of her in the same row. She grabbed the end of the man's lariat and held on as she was forced to run all the way to Brutus's cabin. The men in the next row heard Joe's teeth grinding as he moved ahead on his row of cotton.

When Joe returned from the fields an hour after dark, his son rushed to him. Fetch was now eleven and assigned to a different field than his father, and often finished his field earlier. He was but a scant inch less than six feet tall, and not prone to emotional outbursts, so when he ran crying to Joe, the man was concerned. "Wha the mattuh, son?"

"I had to drag mama to our home, an I think she mebbe dead."

Joe burst through the flimsy door to find his wife lying motionless on their cornhusk sleeping pallet, lying on the floor. When he tried to lift her lifeless body her head rolled to the side and almost all the way around.

• • •

Brutus grabbed Lilly by the hair and thrust her head between his legs, screaming, "You'll do whatever I tell you to do, nigger."

Lilly's pretty face had been repeatedly smashed until it was swollen, but still she managed to speak. "I ain nevah gonna do dat again an I ain nevah comin to you no mo." Her desire to see her son to manhood had been fulfilled, and she was finally broken. She removed the small knife—hidden carefully in her hair. She managed to shove the four inch blade into Brutus' huge belly, but it did little more than further inflame an already raging temper, which had been fueled by whiskey all day. One mighty swing of his gigantic fist and her lovely neck snapped like tinder over his knee. He then grabbed her by the hair and proceeded to drag her outside—knowing that the Colonel was away and his sow was clawing the back of a naked slave. He looked up to see Fetch standing a short distance away with a bucket of water for his family's evening meal. "Fetch this bitch and get her into your quarters." He glared menacingly at the youth until the boy dropped the bucket of water and ran to his mother.

Fetch tried to get Lilly to stand but she seemed more like a sack of flour than his mother. He lifted her into his strong arms and carried her home to await his father's return from the fields. He now sat silent and staring as his father sobbed into the neck of Lilly. When he turned to the boy, there was a look in his dark eyes such as Fetch had never seen. He stood and moved as though he had been transformed into a zombie.

Fetch watched as his father began filling a sack. First went all of his and Lilly's shirts—four. Then items that further confused the boy. With almost all of their possessions inside, the bag was barely half full when he placed it on the dirt floor. He rolled his and Lilly's sleeping pallet back and began digging with a large square nail that he had found and hidden. Several minutes later he held two objects that Fetch had never seen. One was a short machete that Joe had stolen many years earlier when he was first brought from Africa. He carefully removed the piece of oilcloth it was wrapped in, and then wiped the lard from the blade. After laying it on the table he unwrapped a much smaller object—a knife. He wiped the grease from the blade and tested the edge, but still said nothing. With the small knife in his huge hand he moved toward his son who was transfixed as if turned to stone—his mouth hanging open.

"Son, I doan wan you t'be no slave no mo." The boy's eyes were locked onto the blade in his father's hand as he came toward him. "Doan put dis knife in da bag cause you is maybe gone hafta drop da bag an run fo you life, but I gone pray to God fo I leaves dis shack dat He hep you keep it. Here," he held out the knife, "put you han inside dis ledder loop what I fix to da knife, and den hole da knife in you han. Dat way no matter what, you gone have da knife to ketch som'n fo eat. I gone tell you agin son, try to keep de bag cause it gone be a long way till you get to dem Indians what I done tole you about." He leaned forward and assisted Fetch in getting his hand through the leather loop. Joe looked into his son's dark eyes, "You members ever ting what I tole you bout dem Indians what I was tole bout by dem black fellers what was ketch runnin north by Brutus?"

Rick Magers

"Yes, papa, but what about you?"

"Doan worry none bout me, son. You juss take youseff a deep breath an git on outa here an follow dem stars what I showed you so many time. Dey gone lead you to de far south swamp where dem Indians hate dese white mans worse den we does, an dey gone letchew live with them." Tears rolled down his black cheeks as he stared into the darkness of the hovel, and then turned to look at Lilly's dead body. "My dream was we all gone one day run south an live with them Indians, but dat ain gonna be, so you go on now an make me and you mama's dream come true fo you ownseff.

• • •

Thirteen year old Fetch shoved his fears to the back of his mind and moved as swiftly as his long legs would carry him across the land. He was following a map that was drawn on the walls of a very intelligent brain, and maintained by an incredible memory since he was just a small child.

Unless Joe was too exhausted after his long day in the cotton field, he would have his son Fetch follow him to the corner of their hovel. A small candle lit the dirt floor as Joe once again smoothed a small area before handing his son the small pointed stick. Night after night with no variation whatsoever, Joe spoke the same words so softly that only the boy sitting on a short stump of firewood only inches away, could hear. "Draw de map on de flo, son."

Joe's words came out from habit…they weren't necessary. Joe and Lilly had seen evidence of their son's memory while he was still too young to go into the fields and begin his life's work. When Fetch was still called simply Boy, Lilly crawled from beneath the thin blanket and lit their candle. After pulling the tattered dress over her head, she selected a few small sticks to bring life to the smoldering fire inside a lard-tin stove; each slave household's only source of heat and cooking. After stirring the concoction in the cast iron pot, which was each household's only cooking vessel, Lily leaned down and gently rubbed Joe's woolly head until his eyes opened. "Time to fill dat big belly." Her smile helped him begin each day.

Lilly gently stirred the pot as she searched for the carcass of the huge rat that Joe had killed in his cotton row, only yesterday. After gutting the rodent and removing the skin, Lilly had shoved a stick through the prize and held it down inside the tin stove until it was seared, and then she lowered it into the iron pot to simmer with the other ingredients.

After placing the rat on Joe's clay plate, Lilly removed a leg and put it on her son's small clay plate. Using the iron ladle, one of only a few utensils issued to each slave household, she placed carrots, turnips, potatoes, plus two stale bread and flour dumplings on top. Lilly then ladled broth over everything before adding water to the pot so it would be ready for whatever they were lucky enough to bring home at the end of their day.

As Joe settled on one of the tree stumps next to the small table, Lilly went to her son and began gently patting his bare butt. His smile brightened her day as hers did Joe's. Constant hunger motivated each slave to get out of bed quickly in the morning to consume the only food they would have until long after the sun had fallen into the distant trees.

As Joe and Lilly prepared to leave their hovel and head toward the fields with the other slaves, Boy moved unnoticed in the corner. When Lilly turned to remind her son not to leave the hovel until the sun was out, three year old Boy was standing in front of her. On his naked body was his only pair of pants; shortened repeatedly to provide patches for his father's trousers. His tiny hand held one of the spare cotton sacks, and he spoke solemnly as he looked from his mother to his father, "I'se ready to hep wit de work."

Joe smiled slightly as he kneeled down in front of Boy. "Doanchew tink you a bit young fo totin dat cotton bag?"

"Nossir, I gots t'hep you n' mama."

Lilly was instantly on her knees hugging Boy. "Wha fo you tink you gotta come to dem long ole row cotton and work, Boy? You juss a chile what pose to play an have fun."

"Mama, dat nummer three field so big ain no way you an daddy gone be finish fo half d'damn night time," Boy's innocent young eyes looked at his mother, "de way dat stupid damn Brutus make dem rows go dis way an dat way all over dat damn nummer three field, we's gonna hafta keep goin back so we sho ain nuttin miss."

Joe's mouth dropped open and Lilly plopped back on her butt and just stared at her son.

Rick Magers

After tucking the lad back beneath his thin blanket, they headed toward the fields. Joe said quietly; never knowing who was nearby in the darkness, "dat lil feller sho can member things."

He couldn't see it, but Lilly shook her head as she said, "I know Boy got heself a good membry, but dat knock me down. You, an me too, bess watch what we sayin front dat smart lil picaninny, cause he member ever ting we sayin, I tink."

• • •

Fetch took the stick and began carefully drawing the map that would lead him south out of Georgia and toward the Indians who allowed escaped slaves to live among them. Joe looked at his wife lying dead a short distance away, and then turned tear-filled eyes and faced his son, but was forced to swallow before speaking. "Leave dis place tonight and member all da ting I learn you, an if God watchin, He gone hep you fine da way to dem Indian."

After smoothing the packed earth floor where Fetch had drawn the map, Joe stood and embraced his son. Stepping back, Joe said, "I go out an be sho ain no bodies roun to see you go." Five minutes later he returned to see Fetch kneeling beside his dead mother; stroking her hair. "C'mon Boy, time f'you to git away from dis white man's hell." He snuffed the candle and silently opened the door.

As Fetch moved silently through the dark night on his journey toward freedom, his father sat at the small table and watched as the light from the small candle danced across the face of the only woman he had ever loved. Memories of gloriously wonderful days in Africa passed through his mind as he ran the knife's blade back and forth on his muscular, leather-like arm; slowly, carefully sharpening it.

Joe pinched out the candle so their hovel would not be noticed and sat with Lilly through the long night. He wanted his son to have a good head start on the slave trackers, so he waited until just prior to the new day's light arriving above the eastern horizon, and then on bare soundless feet he moved toward Brutus' cabin. Lilly had informed Joe that Brutus was so sure that no slave had the courage to challenge him that he never latched his door. It was left unlatched also for the many women who came to him at all hours to trade their bodies for any small morsel of food that Brutus paid them with.

Rick Magers

Joe eased the cabin's door open on soundless leather hinges, and stepped inside; the razor sharp knife in his hand. He stood against the wall until his eyes grew accustomed to the darkness. When he could finally see the bed outlined by the light of a sliver of moon, he could also see a slight movement just to his left. He turned his head, but the last thing he ever saw was the brilliant explosion of the 10 gauge shotgun that blew his entire head from his body.

Brutus lit his kerosene lantern and looked at Brutus' headless body, and then at what was left of the head. After removing the two spent shells, he shoved two more into the barrels, and leaned the double-barreled shotgun against the wall. "I knowed you'd come to get even and was sittin here all night waitin and grinnin." He poured his tin cup full of whiskey and drank half of it. Still looking at the distorted and mangled head he said, "I'll see to it that Fetch makes up for you and that bitch of yours causing me to lose two good niggers."

A short time after the slaves were in their assigned rows of cotton, Brutus realized that Fetch was gone. He and two slave catchers were soon mounted and following the hounds.

• • •

Fetch was an excellent runner, and had covered a large tract of land before Brutus and his two men were on his trail. He had memorized all of the tactics that the medicine men and elders had learned about eluding the trackers, if an opportunity to escape presented itself. His father had him sit and listen as he quietly explained how to use the items that he would carry with him if ever he could escape. "Boy, I is get dese ting lil by lil, an keep dem bury in rabbit hide. Dis be red pepper an it good fo git dem dog nose all mess up. Ever time you comes to a small river what you can walk cross, lay down an roll all roun on dis side, so dem dog smell you scent real good. Fo you step in day water, put some dis pepper all round where you was rollin, den run long way in dat river fo you climb out. Dem dog mebbe fine where you git out, so put a lil bit mo pepper on da groun. Now, see dis stuff what look like tiny lil rock? Dem old medicine woman make dem, an juss a few mix inside dem rat skin we keep, gone make dem damn hound so sick dey ain gone follow no slave."

While still very young, Boy listened intently as the father he idolized spoke, and he used his incredible memory to categorize all of it away. It the near future it would be called upon to save his life. On and on his father talked; so quietly that even his mother heard very little, but Boy missed nothing, and if he did, he asked...whachew mean, daddy?

• • •

Four days later Brutus and the two men were still pursuing Fetch. The young slave had listened well and learned from his father, and had thrown the dogs off his trail at the first river; just before dark on the day he began his run south. Brutus and his two men camped to allow the hounds to recover, and began again the next morning. As they drank whiskey and rested, Fetch moved cautiously, but steadily south.

At noon the following day the two dogs followed Fetch's scent straight to the four rat hides with the poison balls imbedded inside. He had no way of knowing how many dogs would be after him, so Fetch dropped four...the starving dogs stopped within one hour, and both died by nightfall.

Fetch had moved into North Florida and was brought to a dead stop. Brutus and the two men were still pursuing the property of the Shriff Plantation, but Fetch was several miles ahead of them...standing wide-eyed and staring at the wide Suwannee River. Only the few African tribes, who live near a river that isn't filled with crocodiles, piranhas, or other dangerous creatures, ever learn to swim...Fetch was not one of those. He finally began moving as swiftly as possible through the growth along the bank of the river.

Exhaustion was wearing Fetch down, and now was becoming discouraged by the realization that the men on horses would soon close the gap, and he would be trapped against a river that he could not cross. He began searching for a fallen tree that might be small enough for him to drag into the water and float across on.

Two hours of searching and still nothing small enough for Fetch to drag into the water. He heard the distant whinny of a horse and his heart skipped a beat.

• • •

Unknown to Fetch, several pairs of eyes as dark as his, set deeply into brown faces, had been watching the young black boy since he arrived in their territory. They remained unseen within the dense growth along the river, and moved stealthily along as Fetch had searched for a means to cross the river. They were Indian braves of the Timucua tribe, who called the land in northeast Florida theirs. Escaped slaves were not new to them, but they were puzzled by a boy so young traveling alone. Caution kept the Timucua free and independent during the troubled times that the white men brought to Florida. They approached every situation involving invaders as a possible ploy to enslave them.

When they spotted the three white men riding horses toward the area where the young black boy was still searching for a means to cross the river, they began a series of hand signals and bird calls. They waited until Brutus and the two men turned and rode toward Fetch. "I guess we done found our running nigger." They were to be Brutus' final words. A dozen arrows pierced the three men, and they fell screaming from their saddles. A sharp blade pulled across each wounded man's throat ended their misery. Once the Indians had removed their arrows, they shoved the bodies into the swift current of the river.

Fetch saw what happened and huddled close to the ground. When a young Indian, only slightly older than him, with his long hair made into what Fetch thought looked like a round hat with a topknot, smiled and motioned for him to climb up the bank…Fetch knew that God had been watching over him, and that his slave days had ended.

• • •

Fetch sat behind the young brave as they entered their village on the three horses. Two braves rode double on the other two, and several walked behind while still others followed a mile behind; keeping an eye out for pursuers. They passed through an opening in a log wall that circled the entire village, and was twice as tall as the tallest warrior.

Fetch scanned the village and determined that the larger square building sitting in the middle of many smaller round huts must be the chief's home.

The Timucua had seen many black slaves, and always allowed them to live among them, but this village never had the opportunity to have one live with them. Several young boys and girls approached cautiously to rub Fetch's leg to see if the black was war paint and would come off. They giggled and Fetch smiled down at them. As they walked the horses through the village, the old women saw his smile and knew that he would be an asset to their village.

When the young braves stopped at the large square shelter; covered with palmetto fronds, an old man walked out. He smiled and embraced the young boy who had motioned to Fetch. The boy handed his father the reins of the horse that he and Fetch had arrived on, and the other two braves did likewise. When the boy began talking and motioning toward the black boy, his father, who was the village chief, turned toward Fetch and nodded his head slowly up and down.

Fetch listened intently as the Indians spoke, but could not get the drift of what they were talking about. The Chief accepted the horses, and summoned three young men from the house behind him. His instructions were to slaughter one of the horses so the women could begin preparing it for the evening meal, and to put the other two on pickets so they could graze to get fat and tender.

When the young brave motioned for Fetch to follow him, he smiled at the chief and said thank you for letting me stay here; trying to convey his meaning with hand movement. The old man pointed at the sky and then the earth they stood on before opening his arms wide and moving his head from one end to the other. In sign language he said *the land belongs to everyone*, and then pointed at Fetch and himself. The old man smiled and walked inside his house.

Thirteen year old Fetch followed the young Indian toward a group of Indians; all appearing to be between his age and his new friend's age, which he guessed to be about fifteen. Fetch would be surprised, when months later he learned that his friend, Ohana, was also only thirteen when he helped fire the arrows into Brutus and his men.

The young Timucua braves and girls smiled a friendly greeting as Fetched approached; especially a young maiden wearing only a string of shells and small ornaments around her slender waist. She was attired as the other girls and women were, but had sparkling black eyes set perfectly beneath long black hair that hung down on each side of the most beautiful face that he had ever seen. His breath left him momentarily when he noticed that her eyes danced as she greeted him in her language.

She smiled and placed her finger between two small breasts, which he hardly noticed, since all slave women go bare breasted to the fields; sweat having long ago deteriorated the top of their only dress. She said her name and waited, the bright smile growing wider…"Ata'ahee." He waited patiently, not yet understanding her meaning, until she repeated her name."

"Oh!" Fetch grinned, "Your name is Atahee."

She smiled and shook her head no…**Ata'** she emphasized the first part…ahee…"Ata'ahee."

"Ata' ahee" Fetch smiled and repeated it, "Ata'ahee…very pretty name. She reached forward and touched his bare chest; the shirt long since torn from his body by unseen branches and the like during his long run south. "Fetch" he said and waited.

"Fish." It was common to name the young men for an animal they could catch, imitate, or in some other way be associated with, so Fish seemed an appropriate name for the black boy standing before her. He only tried once more and then smiled and said Fish, pointing at himself. He would learn that it was only a word to the young girl and meant nothing in her language, but since she seemed to like the sound of it…Fish he was that day and Fish he remained during the half century he would live with this tribe of Timucua Indians.

When a friendly black dog moved through the gathering and stopped beside Fish, he intuitively reached down and stroked its ears. The young girl grinned as she saw the dog's tail wagging. She said something that Fish didn't understand, but he realized it was her dog when she pointed at the dog and then at herself; all the while smiling broadly.

Each time she smiled, something odd happened inside Fish that puzzled him. The only girls that he had ever seen to speak to were thin, starving slaves who seldom smiled and never laughed; fearing the whip in Brutus' hand. Fish returned her smile and pointed at the dog and then himself as he rubbed the dog's ears and petted it gently on the head. She smiled again and then moved her hand to the dog's head to pet it, but in the process, touched Fish's hand. After petting the dog, she moved her small brown hand and laid it atop Fish's black hand. A moment later she giggled and moved her hand to pat the dog gently on his back.

The shivers that rushed through his body when the girl touched him, lingered; preventing Fish from speaking or moving. He stood as though turned to stone and stared at the smiling young Indian girl. She once again placed her finger between her breasts and said, "Timucua."

Rick Magers

Fish tried several times when he realized she was telling him what tribe they were. She smiled and said it phonetically while leaving a gap between the two syllables…"tee……moo……qua," and then repeated…tee……moo……qua, before putting it together, "Timucua."

"Tee moo qua." The girl smiled and grabbed his arms to dance him around several times while saying, "Timucua." She then placed her finger on his chest and waited.

"African." Her effort failed and everyone laughed. Fish used her method and said, "Ahh free can." Soon she and her friends were all saying…African. Fish smiled broadly and later followed them to a small creek to swim naked and bathe the day's sweat away.

• • •

Five years passed quickly and Fish was speaking the language of his hosts as though born with it on his tongue. He and young Ata'ahee had become inseparable friends for three years, and lovers for the last two. He had recently gone to her father and asked for her hand in marriage, which he readily agreed to. Fetch had worked hard to prove his worthiness to the Timucua camp, and all were pleased that the two young people had decided to make a life together.

When Fish rode into the Timucua camp sitting on Brutus' horse behind the chief's son, he stood six feet tall…not unusual at all for a Watutsi. His mother, Lilly, was six feet tall in bare feet, which never had shoes on them, and his father, Joe, stood just under seven feet tall the night Brutus surprised him with two barrels holding double ought buckshot.

At eighteen, Fish stood seven feet two inches tall…and was still growing. Chief Outina's son, Chekiki, was unusually tall for a young Timucua brave. He was six and a half feet tall, and with his hair piled high with a top knot sticking straight up, he appeared as tall as Fish. He and Fish formed a silent bond the day five years earlier on the bank of the Suwannee River…a bond that would last their lifetime.

Chekiki's training as a warrior began while he was still a child. His three uncles devoted many hours each day as they took turns taking the child into the forests and swamps to teach him the wild ways of the world into which he had been born. By the time he was five he could hear a rattlesnake moving through the brush long before his uncles.

His incredible hearing was equaled by eyesight that easily detected movement long before others saw a thing.

He learned every faucet of survival in the wilds of Northeast Florida, and patiently instructed his new black African friend. At fifteen, each of them, along with several boys the same age, were put under the tutelage of legendary War Chief Saturiwa's nephew, who had married into Chief Outina's tribe.

Fish soon learned that Chekiki also had a good memory; never needing to be told anything a second time—once learned, available for life. Together, this group of young men learned stalking, ambush, hand to hand combat with only one survivor when the enemy was real, tool making, medicinal plants to eat or treat wounds to stop bleeding, how to quickly set deadly traps to injure a pursuing enemy…and all of the needed skills to either attack an enemy camp, or defend their own.

One year after beginning, their instructor informed Chief Outina that he had fourteen new warriors who were trained and ready to fight if called upon. He added, to the great pleasure of the old chief, that his son and the black boy were the best two that he had ever taught.

In a very short time they would have the opportunity to prove that their instructor was correct.

• • •

Three months after the ceremony, held traditionally to initiate young men as warriors, a small band of renegade Apalachee Indians began moving east from their territory in the panhandle area of Northwest Florida. Fifty rambunctious young warriors decided they would find a new area in which to live with their wives and children, where game was more plentiful.

They moved steadily east until they entered a new area…land that for centuries belonged to the Timucua Indians. They scouted ahead and bypassed two large Timucua villages, which appeared to have a population of over five hundred. One hundred and fifty miles from their home village they were nearing Chief Outina's village in the area of what years later would become Lake City.

Unknown to the band of Apalachee, the Timucua kept scouts out in the forest and marshes constantly. Their sole purpose was to spot any groups of people, white, brown, black—warriors or otherwise, who were moving about on Timucua land.

Rick Magers

Chief Outina listened intently as his lead scout told of what he had seen only two day's walk from the village. He told his son to assign six new scouts to go with the scout who had brought the news, and to relieve those who had been out for three days. "Tell them to send runners by nightfall to advise me about the Apalachee." He then summoned his War Chief and told him to bring his sub chiefs to council. Two hours later their meeting was terminated and they began organizing three groups of twenty warriors each to prepare an ambush, and another three groups of ten each to set up the defense of their village. Within one hour, the twenty warriors left the village at a run. They spread out a quarter mile apart, but moved as one unit as they neared the area where they planned to ambush the enemy. The scouts had informed the chief that the Apalachee were adorned in red scarves and had their faces painted red…the color of war.

There was now a line of sixty Timucua warriors stretching across the obvious path that the enemy would take while advancing toward the Timucua village. Fish and Chekiki set their bundles holding short pointed sticks on the ground. Each warrior passed by and was given a handful of the sticks and immediately began burying them with the sharpened end facing the enemy. After camouflaging them with leaves they began hanging small fish hooks stolen from the Spanish at the fort in St. Augustine.

Soon, many of the branches hanging low were filled with hooks tied with fishing line; also stolen from the Spaniards. Fish and several other warriors carefully checked the entire area to be certain that their ambush was not noticeable, and then worked their way through the hooks and sticks, to find a good position of concealment and wait for their scouts to arrive.

The sound of a hawk alerted the line of hidden warriors that men were approaching. When Fish spotted their scouts in the distance, he sent the trilling of a blue jay toward them. The six scouts stopped and waited until Chekiki and Fish came to lead them through the ambush.

The War Chief stood silently and listened as the lead scout told him about the advance of the Apalachee and how many they were. He looked through the dense forest cover to locate the sun. "They will be here when the sun is straight overhead."

Fish grinned, displaying his pure white teeth, made more so by the contrast of his black face. "And here is where they will stay."

Rick Magers

The War Chief liked Fish and returned his grin, "We must be careful not to kill them all, because we want a few to return and tell their chief that it will be wise to never again go against the mighty Timucua." The warriors gathered around him nodded their heads, and then began searching for more material to conceal themselves from the enemy.

Fish spotted the red headgear before he saw the warrior wearing it. He glanced up and saw the sun, directly overhead, shining through the trees. He thought; *Aku-Saturiwa is a wise war chief*...his eyes moved back and forth across the warriors approaching...*these men are moving too fast through an area as dense as this...they must be young men trying to prove their bravery.*

There was no movement whatsoever among the Timucua as the enemy warriors approached. When several rammed their fast moving feet into the sharpened sticks, and others were struggling to unsnarl their clothing from the fish hooks, sixty-six Timucua warriors stood and unleashed a barrage of arrows into the Apalachee braves—standing only thirty feet away.

So effective was their sticks and hooks, that not one Timucua warrior was even wounded, although a few Apalachee were able to fire a few arrows and spears. In less than ten minutes, forty-one Apalachee were either dead or wounded so severely that they could only watch helpless as the Timucua cut the throats of their friends who were moaning nearby. The remaining few were not pursued—as War Chief had decreed.

All of the dead were scalped but five. Their hair was left as it was, and taken to the Timucua village—with their head. All of the scalps and the five Apalachee heads would soon be hanging from tall posts encircling Chief Outina's council fire.

● ● ●

Fish and Chekiki sat near each other on the night of the successful ambush. The central cooking fire had fresh horse, alligator, snapping turtle, venison, opossum, one small brown bear and several raccoons attached to wooden smoking racks. A great victory against a worthy opponent called for a great feast. Chief Outina praised his war chief, who in turn praised his warriors. The women had brewed a special herbal tea, which is the traditional drink of the Timucua, and were circulating among the men with gourds and conch shells full of the heady brew. It is a concoction so strong, commented a Frenchman visiting a Timucua village, that even in the absence of alcohol, it still makes a person unused to it, light headed and somewhat tipsy.

One by one the warriors stood and told stories of bravery; not their own, but the courageous, cunning, and skillful deeds of their fellow warrior friend.

Chekiki stood and told how his blood brother Fish, stood tall and in plain view as the Apalachee charged toward them. "Whoosh, whoosh, whoosh," he said, imitating the arrows leaving Fish's bow, "my brother fired all of his arrows and then threw all three of his spears, and," he said grinning, "I saw several warriors fall to the ground screaming." Chekiki pantomimed the shooting of arrows and throwing imaginary spears, "My arrows and spears were used, so when Fish was finished, we both moved forward and began finishing the enemy off with our knives." He pointed to a head hanging from a post, "Fish cut the man loose from his body and brought it to our chief."

After a few warriors had stood to praise their friend, Fish stood. "I will always fight hard for my people, but all that I have learned came from my brother Chekiki. When we were but children, he was already a seasoned warrior and I a slave running frightened through the woods. He helped kill my white pursuers, and then allowed me to ride behind him on my enemy's horse. From that day until my last breath, I will do my very best to defend him, this village, and my new family…the Timucua." He sat down and then smiled as everyone chanted several times…Fish, Fish, Fish.

• • •

Fish and Chekiki lay beneath feather-light blankets of camouflaged material sewed together by the women of their village. They were no longer young men…now in their mid thirties and at the peak of their physical endurance and mental capabilities. All who knew these two men realized that they had extraordinary memory skills and could return from a scouting mission with every detail they had witnessed.

Chief Outina chose his son Chekiki and the black warrior to be his eyes; he was rapidly aging and could no longer go on reconnaissance. "I want you two warriors to watch the tin soldiers at the place they call

Fort Augustine. Stay long enough to understand if what I have been told by the traveling white traders is true; that these strange men who wear tin are capturing our people and forcing them to be slaves." The old man noticed Fish's eyes become hard and his lips smaller at the mention of that word. "If it is true, then we must meet with the chief's of all Timucua and decide what to do."

Before Chekiki could speak to his father, Fish said, "Mighty Chief Outina, we will learn all that you need to deal with these strange men. I and Chekiki have watched from the trees when they moved about the land, and they are a cruel people."

"Yes," Chekiki spoke up, "we have watched many times as they pass beneath us, and they are even cruel to each other. A chief on a white horse shoved his long knife through the neck of one of the soldiers in tin clothes."

Fish nodded and said, "They will be an easy enemy to kill. They make so much noise moving through a forest that we have half of the day to prepare our ambush after we first hear them."

On the third day of watching the Spaniards, Fish and Chekiki saw a long line of Timucua Indians being marched into the Spanish fort. Their hands were secured behind and a long rope stretched from the brave in front to the squaw in the very rear. Each captive was secured to the long rope by a smaller one wrapped around their waist.

After dark the two warriors slipped away and began the long run through the night to reach their village. The distance to their village, deep within the dense forest north of the future Lake City, was eighty miles. If the moon had been in the dark phase, they would not have been able to move across the land so swiftly, but a full moon lit the way, and they covered enough during the first night to allow them to complete their journey in three more days.

They set a pace running through the long daylight hours; still ever alert to danger, but moving swiftly across the rugged terrain. When darkness arrived they continued ahead, but slowed their pace to match the area they were in. Several white immigrants had moved into the inner areas to escape religious persecution by the Catholic Spaniards, who were establishing settlements all along the coast near Ft. Augustine. The Timucua Indians traded occasionally with these tough people, but Fish and Chekiki knew it was very dangerous to move too close through an area where they had settled, because they had guards watching all day and all night. The two warriors could spot one of the settlements far in advance, by the alien smells during the day and their small lanterns at night.

Fish and Chekiki took turns being the front-runner; giving the forward scout's eyes time to rest. Just prior to dark on the second day, it paid off. Chekiki was fifty feet ahead of Fish when his incredible eyesight noticed a very slight movement in a large oak tree with low hanging limbs. He slowed slightly and raised his arm—a signal to Fish of danger ahead.

Without missing a stride Fish slowed his pace to match that of his friend and pulled a long hunting arrow from the sheath slung across his black muscular back, and notched it to the bow that he worked many long hours to perfect. He had become the best archer among all of the Timucua braves in his village, and his dark eyes were now piercing the coming darkness to see what Chekiki had seen. The arrow was pulled half way back as he closed the gap, and the moment that his friend was beneath the limbs of the huge oak, Fish pulled the arrow all the way back and moved cautiously ahead.

Chekiki had complete confidence in his friend's ability to understand the situation, and without glancing up he moved on beneath the tree. Fish spotted the movement in the shadows and brought his arrow toward the huge cougar, which was perched overhead and ready to pounce on his evening meal—Chekiki.

So intent was the lion, and so silent was Fish, that the beast never knew of the danger until the long arrow pierced its heart. As the big cougar lost its footing and life simultaneously, and began the twelve-foot fall to the ground, Fish notched another arrow and had it pulled back by the time the animal hit the ground.

They rested that night; exhausted from a run spanning a full night and the following day. After a meal of dried meat and fresh berries that they picked along the way, each took a drink from his animal bladder waterbag. "You sleep," Fish said to his friend, "I watch first."

"Thank you, I'm tired. Wake me when the moon has traveled half way across the sky."

• • •

Two days of running later, as the sun fell into the forest to begin darkening the day, Fish and Chekiki trotted into their village. After a warm welcome from their wives and friends, they proceeded to Chief

Outina's square house. The old chief welcomed his son and Fish home and then sent two runners to summon his sub-chief and war chief to council. Chief Outina's oldest wife began brewing a batch of her special herbal tea to help Fish and Chekiki regain their strength. It was ready when the two chief's arrived, and all of the men accepted a gourdful. The three chief's sat silently sipping as the two warriors told what they had seen.

"These men are very strange," Chekiki said, "It is hot and there was not even a breeze from the big water, and yet they all wear the tin clothes over other clothes made from what looked like heavy cloth." He shook his head vigorously and his round topknot wiggled.

Fish waited five years for his kinky hair to grow long enough for his wife, Ata'ahee, to weave it atop his head in a traditional Timucua headdress. He was an impressive figure as he sat beside Chief Outina with his black head over a foot higher and his hair woven carefully into a round roll that circled his head before being pulled up to the top and manipulated into the topknot—traditional Timucua headdress. It resembled a modern wool seaman's stretch cap with the bottom edge rolled up, with a tassel on top. Fish was very proud of Ata'ahee for being able to create such a striking headdress for him with only half as much hair as the other warriors had.

"My chief," Fish began while looking at Outina, "everything we observed about these tiny men who wear strange clothing, makes me believe they are evil. They had two Apalachee men tied to poles like these," he pointed to the poles near the fire where the heads of the six Apalachee warriors had been hanging years earlier. "A tin chief and two tin soldiers tortured the two men for two days, but we do not believe that they got the information they wanted from them. Chekiki and I watched as the tin soldiers cut the two Apalachee into many pieces. Perhaps it was because the tin soldiers have no women and this is entertainment for them?" He shrugged his wide shoulders, "If we rid the world of them it will be a good thing we do."

Chief Outina stood and shouted a command, and a young warrior stepped from the darkness. "Call all of my runners." The youth departed in a blur and within minutes a dozen young runners arrived. "Go swiftly now to all nearby Timucua villages and inform their chief that we face danger and must all meet in this many days," he held up both hands and folded in the thumbs; leaving all eight fingers erect, "at Chief Saturiwa's big village near the grassy lake."

Rick Magers

The twelve young men departed in separate directions to carry their chief's message throughout the local Timucua nation. In eight days all of the local Timucua chiefs and their escorts were gathered in the great Chief Saturiwa's huge village near a large lake a short distance from modern Gainesville.

Fish had never met the chief of all thirty local Timucua villages. He was honored when Chief Saturiwa walked directly to him, and spoke. "I have long heard of the tall black warrior who chose to live with my people, and I am pleased to see that they did not exaggerate your size." He smiled warmly and then continued, "We are a very peaceful people, but when we must fight we are as fierce as a lion that has been pushed to the edge of water. I am told that you have proven yourself to be a very fierce and fearless warrior."

Fish looked into the man's eyes and liked what he saw—honesty. The chief was tall for a Timucua, standing only slightly shorter that Fish. "King Saturiwa, I will always fight for the people who saved my skinny little black ass when I was just a child."

"Ha, ha, ha, I like the plain way you speak, but I am not the king of our people," he smiled again, "even though my people enjoy calling me king. A true king will one day rule over our people as one, but when he arrives he will be a much greater man than I." He reached out and patted Fish on the shoulder, and motioned toward the gathered chiefs of all thirty tribes that he was responsible for. "Come and let me tell the others who you are."

Fish followed the great man, but was a bit weak at the knees to be so honored. He was surprised to learn, that to a man, the chief's had all heard about him.

• • •

The decision was made to form a war group to attack the Spaniards at Fort Augustine before they had captured more Timucua to be made into slaves. Any that were still there would be freed and given weapons with which to help in the battle. The chiefs of the thirty villages would select the group, and Chief Saturiwa would choose the leaders from his own men.

Thirty days after the war council at Chief Saturiwa's village, over twelve hundred Timucua warriors had stealthily moved to within five miles of Fort Augustine. It was set up as a three pronged assault, with a separate and very special group of six select warriors led by Fish to sneak in at night and locate any Timucua that had survived their imprisonment. Each warrior carried a package containing steel knives, bartered from the traveling white traders. "We must make contact with our brothers and sisters and tell them to wait until they hear the main group rushing in at dawn when our men have opened the big doors." Fish looked at each of his six men, who nodded their silent agreement. "Tell them to sever their bonds, and as they head toward the big doors, kill as many of the little men as they can." Fish looked at the darkening sky before adding, "We will leave here when the sliver of moon has traveled half way across the sky."

Chekiki also had been given a special task and four warriors to perform it. Their mission was far more dangerous than the one given to Fish and his men. Chief Saturiwa summoned his friend's son, and when he arrived, beckoned Chekiki to sit with him. "Outina tells me that you are as silent as a hungry alligator stalking its dinner." The old legendary chief smiled and called for his wife to bring more tea.

"I learned everything from my father and hope to some day be as good a warrior as he is."

"From his own lips you already are." The chief sipped his scalding hot tea before continuing. "It is vital to the success of our initial assault on the fort where the small men live, that we know where they will be sleeping and also where their chiefs will be."

Without hesitation, Chekiki answered. "I will chose four warriors from our village who can slip between a man and his woman without either knowing it." He grinned at the old man when he heard him chuckling.

Chief Saturiwa smiled and said, "I am very glad that those men did not live in my village when I was a young man."

Chekiki smiled, but then became very serious when he spoke. "We will bring your chiefs the information they need, and the little tin men will never know they were being watched."

• • •

Beneath a sliver of moon, Fish and his men moved silently toward the rear wall of the fort. Scouts had earlier climbed into the highest branches of the large oaks surrounding the fort a hundred yards distant.

They informed Chief Saturiwa that there were at least fifty captives penned against the wall in the southeast corner.

As Fish and his men advanced to the area where they now knew there were captive slaves, Chekiki and his man were silently climbing the poles that the Spaniards constructed the fort's outer walls with. The four men he had chosen were the best climbers, and could follow Chekiki into the highest branches of the largest oaks, but more importantly they were able to perform these feats with the silence of a snake stalking its dinner.

Fish and his six men moved to within a few feet of the area where the captives were held and waited. Each warrior began removing a slender vine rope from his waist. They then tied the rope to the seven bundles that held the small sharp knives. When they finished, they sat back on their haunches and waited for the Spaniards to finish drinking wine and telling stories while staggering around a large fire in the middle of the courtyard.

Chekiki climbed to the top and peeked over, but quickly returned to his men on the ground. "They are drinking," he whispered, "which is good."

Two hours later the fire was burning down. Fish moved to the wall and placed his eye against the slight crack between the vertical logs. He could see that several of the captives had shifted enough to lean back against the wall. He moved silently to that area and began probing gently with the long thin tree branch that he cut earlier. After several tries, the branch was suddenly stopped, but then it was shoved back and forth. He had located the widest crack and now placed his lips to it and whispered, "We have come to save you and kill these tin men." The branch was vigorously pulled back and forth. Fish smiled, *I must have found the smartest warrior among them.*

Chekiki and his four men were all at the top of the wall, clinging to the outside with toes and fingers. Ten minutes of watching and they knew exactly which buildings the men and their chief's went to for sleep. They silently came down and as planned, immediately headed toward the area where the Timucua waited.

Fish and his men leaned a stout ten-foot long pole they had carried with them, against the wall. The youngest of his men grasped all seven lines and deftly climbed to the top of the wall as two others steadied the pole. Cautiously the youth peeked over and saw that there were no guards watching the captives. He scanned the compound and spotted only two guards walking on a plank walkway that ran across the inside of the front wall, which faced the forest. He made the faintest clicking noise by popping his tongue against the roof of his mouth, a signal common to the Timucua.

Very slowly a young man below him turned his head until his eyes could scan the area where the noise came from. The warrior on the pole outside pulled one of the bundles up and lowered it to the ground. A woman leaning against the wall reached out and pulled it to her. One by one each bundle of knives and some dried meat were lowered to the captives.

Fish returned to the area where he had probed with the stick. He placed his eye to the large gap again, and saw the man turn briefly toward him and then turn away and nod his head. He very slowly scooted backwards while watching the two guards. When he was finally leaning against the wall, Fish whispered. "Sever the ropes but wait until our warriors have opened the big doors at dawn. We are six hundred and have come to free you, and also wipe out these devils. A hundred warriors will be against the side walls when the doors open, and as they rush in, the others will be charging from the forest."

Fish heard simply a whispered, "yes." By the hard determination in the voice, he realized that the captives had not given up hope of somehow being rescued. Fish grinned as he returned to his six men. They all moved away from the wall and sat down to await the sun's arrival. As a faint light showed on the eastern horizon, four Timucua warriors silently climbed the wall and entered the fort. Moments later, the two sentries, groggy from last night's wine, briefly felt a thin sharp blade touch their neck. Their bodies were quietly lowered to the plank they had been walking back and forth on, and the warriors opened the huge gates to Fort Augustine. The Spaniards were about to suffer a fate that would shock the Spanish empire for many years.

When the hundred warriors, who were pressed against the north and south walls, heard the loud trilling screech of an eagle, they rushed around the corner and entered to fort. At the same time, when the war chief's heard the signal, they led the mass of warriors on the short run toward the fort. In the lead were fifty men, each carrying a bundle of dry kindling. Behind then was another fifty with flaming pine-pitch torches. There were no shouts or war screams as they entered Fort Augustine, but the thundering noise of over a thousand feet slamming into the ground, woke several Spanish officers who had remained sober the night before.

In the short time required for the Spanish officers to climb into their uniform and buckle the belt holding their sword, the men carrying the kindling had placed it in pre-determined areas...the front of the two building where the soldiers and officers slept...against the walls of several smaller buildings...and along the inside of the fort's walls. When the officers were appropriately dressed for battle, the front of their sleeping quarters was already engulfed in flames. They yelled to their comrades, who were by this time trying to get their uniforms on, and then rushed through the flames to find hundreds of Timucua warriors, painted in traditional red war paint, standing in a line with their arrows notched and ready.

The soldiers in the enlisted men's quarters took longer to grasp the situation—their heads still cloudy from alcohol. When the commotion began, they stumbled around in the darkness—accomplishing nothing. When the flames were noticeable beneath the door, and smoke began entering, their panic added a fatal note to their plight. Only five made it out the door before the flames made it impossible for the remaining hundred soldiers. The five Spaniards stood in their under garments, looking and acting like sheep, as they were slaughtered.

One of the five was huge, which caused Fish to recall the days when Brutus abused him and killed his mother. The man did not resemble Brutus...except in Fish's memory. He stared hard at the man standing dumbfounded on the burning porch, and screamed in English, a language he hadn't used in many years...**Brutus**. Fish dropped his bow and charged the man, holding only his knife. The Spaniard turned toward the black man who was screaming as he came at him. He raised the sword that he intuitively grabbed as he ran from the burning bunkhouse, but it was in vain. Fish pulled the blade across the man's throat, and the sword dropped to the porch and bounced on to the ground. Fish plunged the blade into the Spaniard's heart as he stared into the dead eyes. "That is for my dear mother." He shoved the huge Spaniard into the flames and looked around to see if there were any others who had escaped...there were none.

Ten minutes after the Timucua entered the fort, all of the captives were outside and being escorted to the area where a hundred warriors had remained in reserve. Chief Saturiwa approached his War Chief and spoke quietly to him, "These people have suffered greatly at the hands of the tin men, and from what they told us, it appears that your men have everything under control, so have these warriors that you held in reserve escort them to my village." He turned and walked to the captives then spoke to the man who appeared to be the strongest among them. "Go with these warriors to my village where you can be fed, and in a few days you will be escorted back to your own villages."

The large man who had stepped forward earlier to tell Chief Saturiwa where the Spaniards had captured them, now bowed to him. "Mighty King Saturiwa, we will always remember that you came in great numbers to save us from the terrible men in iron clothes." He continued bowing until the chief placed his hand on his head and spoke quietly to him.

"You are all Timucua and we must always help each other if we are to survive the invasion by these devils. Now go and be fed by my village."

• • •

The fort burned to the ground, and when, several months later, five Spanish ships arrived to re-supply Fort Augustine, the men were aghast at finding the bones of their countrymen, scattered amongst the ashes of their once grand fort.

The comandante wasted little time mourning the loss of his friends. He ordered the small fleet to head south while the weather was good. In a few days they had unloaded their supplies at Fort Matanzas and were on the way home to Spain, where they would sound the alarm to alert the government that armed aggression had been raised in New Spain to run them out.

When the full Spanish Armada arrived on the coast of North Florida the following year, it was the beginning of the end for the ancient Timucua Indians. So systematic was their slaughter of not only the Timucua, but the Apalachee in the panhandle as well, that both tribes were soon extinct.

• • •

Rick Magers

For two difficult years, Chief Aku-Saturiwa and all of the other chiefs, led the once peaceful Timucua Indians into battle with the invading Spaniards. They no longer had a home village. They were a people constantly on the run as they used guerilla tactics on the soldiers of an enraged Spanish Empire. When they killed one hundred Spanish soldiers there were soon five hundred new soldiers to take their fallen comrades place. The Timucua were soon only ten percent of what they had been prior to attacking Fort Augustine…the end was near and Chief Saturiwa and all of the others knew it.

Outina summoned his son Chekiki, who was now chief, and his new War Chief, Fish. Both men sat beside him as the fire warmed their weary bones, and drank strong herbal tea. "We will soon follow our brothers and sisters to the afterlife unless we gather what people we have left and leave this place to the tin men." He sipped his tea and waited.

Finally Chief Chekiki spoke. "Where can we go, father?"

Outina placed his empty gourd on the ground and turned his head toward the south as he quietly spoke. I have talked to the white traders about the area at the end of land. It is a place where no white man can go and there are no people living there. There are many stories told about creatures who roam the vast, wet, grassy prairies looking for food and they will eat anything. There are places so dense with trees that a snake must stay in one tree all his life because it cannot move. I believe we will have a very hard time living there," the old man turned to his new chiefs, and looked hard into their eyes, "but we will certainly all die if we remain here."

• • •

The move south was discussed with all of the remaining Timucua, which, due to disease and starvation, was now less than one hundred. All agreed that the men in tin clothes would not rest until every one of them was dead.

The small band of Timucua Indians who had lived in Northeast Florida for centuries were led into the Everglades by Chief Chekiki and Chief Fish, the only black Timucua. Their small band of Native Americans now numbered less than forty, but was determined to survive—and they did.

Rick Magers

During the next two hundred years they multiplied slowly, due to the harsh conditions in which they had chosen to live, rather than die at the hands of the invading white men.

As the white men pushed farther and farther into South Florida, the scattered tribes of Native Americans began following the example set earlier by the Timucua, and moved into the Everglades, where the white men still did not go.

Natural conditions, such as the ever-present mosquitoes and other bugs, caused all of the tribes to adopt certain uniform habits. One that all tribes quickly accepted was wearing several layers of light clothing, to keep the bugs and mosquitoes from feasting on their flesh.

The Timucua soon realized that the tall bun of hair was hindering their movement through dense growth as they stalked game. Braves were soon wearing their hair hanging down tight to the side of their head.

Women forsake their comfortable nakedness when they first encountered the voracious mosquitoes and maddening sand flies. Soon the Muskogee and Creek Indians were fleeing the invading white men, and moving into the Everglades of South Florida.

• • •

Both Chekiki and Fish lived to be old men. They created separate villages but kept in touch and learned together to hunt animals new to them, and catch fish they had never seen. Ata'ahee provided Fish with seven sons and five daughters. All found mates in nearby villages, but moved back to live with their families in the village of the black Chief Fish.

Chief Chekiki matched his lifelong friend in sons, but outdid him in daughters; having his sixth when he was seventy-seven, and his seventh and last when he was eighty.

Both men lived with one woman their entire lives, and provided their villages with good leadership until they turned it over to their oldest son when he had proven himself wise enough to be chief.

THE END

Rick Magers

9

GLYN MacCRIMMON
&
THE APACHE

The horse and mule sensed the rattler before they were within striking range. Glyn MacCrimmon was so involved with his bagpipes, that he didn't sense the pace of his horse slowing down. The viper didn't hear a note as the pipes blared loudly for all the world to hear, but it did feel the vibrations as the eight hooves touched down—much to near his lair.

The old rattler moved back against the rear of the small boulder. A desert varmint had previously hollowed out a small area beneath one edge, and with the intense heat of the summer noon sunshine only a short time away; the rattler moved in. Once coiled against the boulder's coolness, the rattler patiently waited for late afternoon; when it would begin hunting for food.

The first vibrations disturbed it's resting, when the two animals were still a quarter mile away. The viper began probing with its forked tongue, and soon realized that the vibrations were coming directly toward his temporary lair. The rattler's five foot of body was soon coiled tightly and ready to strike. It had flexed its mouth several times to be certain that the venom gland was full and ready. The tip of the tail was out of the coil and protruding slightly above, but the rattles remained silent.

Fifteen minutes later the horse began sensing danger. The old mule had carried packs across this area of the Arizona desert before, and he was always tuned in to danger—especially from rattlesnakes. The mule began slowing, which made the line that was tied to a ring at the rear of the horse's saddle get tight.

Mac, which was all anyone ever called him during the fifty years he had been in Arizona, noticed the difference in his horse's gait. He turned to see why, and noticed the taught rope.

It was at that exact moment that the rattler lunged out and made a strike at the horse's leg…hoping no doubt to spook it and cause the animal to change direction.

It worked—the horse reared up on its rear legs and Mac was thrown out of the saddle…still clutching his sacred set of bagpipes. At sixty he could still break a wild horse if the need arose, and took great joy in occasionally proving it. With great dexterity of motion, which any younger rider would have applauded, Mac aligned his long legs beneath him and landed on both feet…housed in size 13 boots. Clutching the pipes under his huge arm, he waved the other arm as a balancing pole and quickly regained his footing. After looking for a snake, which he felt sure, was the only animal that could spook ole Bladder without making a sound, he gently laid the pipes at his feet.

Mac pulled the makings of a smoke from his shirt pocket; as he scanned the area in search of his beloved, record making horse, which if 'coaxed a wee bit with a few beers' according to Mac, 'can piss five gallons without stopping'…hence the name he'd carried for eighteen years.

Bladder had stopped about a hundred yards from the snake's lair, and having no say in the matter, the mule did too. Mac waved his hat and called until he was horse himself. Bladder and the mule just stood and looked in the direction of Mac, who placed his left hand on his hip and glared at Bladder…his thoughts evil, *if I 'ad that bloody rifle in me hand, you hard headed jackass posing as a horse, I'd shoot you from here n' ride that bloody mule to California.*

Bladder continued looking as the mule nibbled at weeds and small flowers. Mac glared and shook his ham size fist in the air, but finally gave up and sat down on a boulder…after checking to be sure there wasn't another rattler beneath it. He'd seen the big rattler moving fast across the boulders, and knew it was holed up a good ways from the intruders, but he pulled his Colt from its holster and yelled loudly, so Bladder could hear. "**I see you by Jesus, you goddamned rattler.**" He fired twice in the air and returned the revolver to the holster, then walked a short distance, while unbuckling his leather belt and easing it out of the loops on his pants…so Bladder wouldn't see him doing it. Mac bent down and came up with the belt hanging from his hand—like a snake. He held it out so the horse could see it, and then tossed it up and out away from him, while yelling loudly…**got the sneaky son uvabitch, Bladder…c'mon boy, and bring Mule with ya.**

He turned and headed toward a mass of huge boulders that had created a small hill during an earthquake sometime in the past; bending down swiftly to retrieve his belt. *He'll be here, fore to bloody long. Stupid beast can't get along without me and better'n I can without him.*

Mac walked the hundred or so yards to the pile of boulders without once turning to see if the horse was coming…he knew it would. When Mac passed the small boulder and approached the one that was almost as large as his cabin back in Nogales, he stopped dead in his tracks.

The Apache was leaning back against a boulder damn near as big as the one that had his left leg pinned. The Indian sitting there didn't surprise Mac nearly as much as the fact that he was just calmly looking straight into Mac's eyes. He moved slowly toward the man and grinned, then spoke in the Chiricahua dialect, which was the language that his dress indicated. "Are you just resting, old warrior?"

"Yes! I will be leaving when the sun gets low and it is not so hot."

Mac stopped beside him and squat down. He looked at the part of the leg not beneath the boulder then at the Apache. "Gonna take that leg with you when you leave?"

"I do not think so, at least not all of it."

Mac looked deeply into the black eyes, and saw three things, which he seldom saw in any white man's eyes…wisdom, curiosity, and strength, but neither pain nor helplessness—although he knew both must be present. Mac pulled his chewing tobacco pouch from his shirt pocket, and after pulling off a chunk, tore it in half and held one to the Indian.

Rick Magers

"Thank you; I have not had this in a long time."

Mac nodded and replaced the pouch, then began working his into the corned of his mouth. When it was where it belonged, he asked the man, "When did the boulder fall on your leg?"

"Did you feel the ground rumbling this morning?"

"No, but Bladder did, and stopped. Wouldn't budge for a helluva long time. I saw some rocks and small boulders falling and knew it was Mother Nature rearranging her furniture."

The Indian laughed quietly and said, "I never heard that before, but maybe it is true."

"Is that when the boulder fell on your leg?"

"It only shifted a little, but when something this big changes its sleeping position, the land changes much." He looked toward the horse and mule, where they were grazing on what little there was to remove the nagging hunger from their empty bellies. "You named the horse Bladder?"

"Yep! Been with me since he was a colt." Mac was surprised that he understood English, and amazed at how calmly the old Apache conversed with him…as if they were old pals and had stopped during a casual walk.

"Why you name him Bladder?"

" 'Cause he kin piss a bucketful big enough to drown a full grown sheep in."

"Umph!" The Indian grunted, "He would be very valuable when it is time to cure the hides."

Mac removed his homemade leather hat and went forward to rest on his knees to have a better look at the half buried leg. "That's what I use it for." He used his fingers, covered on the end with nails that were as hard and durable as steel, to probe a sandy looking area beneath the exposed kneecap. He heard a noise and turned to see Bladder towing a reluctant mule. Mac brushed his huge leathery hands together then looked at the Apache. "Bladder bolted when a rattler came lunging out over there." He nodded with his head toward the area he'd just come from…his long, bright red hair shook.

"What do you put on your hair to make it red like that? I would like to have red hair."

Without cracking a smile, Mac answered, "Gotta wash it in horse piss every day for a year and pack it in horse shit every night with a bandana over it."

Rick Magers

"If I get back to my people, I will do it."

Mac stopped and sat back on his haunches. "Nah! Don't do that. I was just talking and being a smart ass. Where my daddy was born, a lot of people, wimmin too, have red hair the day they're born."

The Apache grinned, "You think I believed you? I would not be called shithead, even for red hair. Where your father born?"

Mac chuckle before answering, "A place far away and across a large water. I was born there too, but came with my family to live here. It is called Scotland, and I hope some day to return and be buried there." He stood and headed toward Bladder, who was now standing next to the mule, a few yards away. He returned with a small shovel and a short handle pick. He got back on his knees and carefully began excavating beneath the Apache's leg. "Where were you born?"

"I was a Bedonkohe Apache when I was born over there in that country." He pointed toward what would one day soon become New Mexico. "I am the grandson of the great Chief Mahko. Was your father a chief in the land where he was born?"

Mac took a break from digging and wiped the sweat from his broad forehead. "No, he was a man who worked the land, and loved what he did for the few things he was able to provide for his family's table."

"He was a wise man. Only the wise ones understand the reason to remain close to the land." He leaned forward and watched as Mac resumed digging. "Will the leg have to come off?" His matter-of-fact tone was more curiosity than apprehension…it caused Mac to stop for a moment to answer.

"If I can get it out from under this boulder before too much longer, and get some blood circulating, I think it will be a good leg again." He paused a moment before adding, with a smile toward the Apache, "A wee bit crooked mebbe, but a good leg never-the-less."

The man smiled back, "I will get used to a crooked leg much quicker that I would no leg."

Mac returned to digging and scratching, as he talked occasionally to the Apache. "The only reason this here leg wasn't squashed like a Bessie Bug under a horse hoof is 'cause there was a lotta sand blowed up agin the boulder. You're already gittin some blood circulating in it, 'cause the color's come back a little, since I got some of the pressure off the damn thing, but I got all of the sand dug out and am now in hard packed stuff that's gonna take some time." Mac put the shovel aside and chipped at the granite-like earth holding the Indian's leg trapped against the huge boulder.

The noonday sun had moved very near the western mountains, but Mac continued chipping. He stopped only long enough to get he and the Apache some cougar jerky and the water bag to wash it down with.

As the horizon began turning gray, the Apache commented quietly, "My leg feels like a tribe of small ants are walking on it."

"That's good. The leg is lose and now all I gotta do is get your foot lose and we'll gitcha out from under this damn rock."

Barely minutes from the lights being turned off for the night, Mac was able to ease the Apache's leg from beneath the boulder. After dragging the Apache away from the boulders, in the event another earthquake decided to shake the ground, Mac quickly gathered enough firewood to get a good fire going, and then prowled with a torch until he had accumulated enough wood to keep it going all night.

He handed the man another two strips of cougar and the bag of water, and then straddled the injured leg and began vigorously massaging it to get blood circulating through it again. He looked up and asked, "The ants leaving yet?"

"Yes! Only a few are still dancing on my foot."

Another half hour of massaging and Mac stood. "I still got a little grain for Bladder and that mule, so I better give 'em some. Don't want one of 'em to drop dead of starvin…gonna need 'em both if we're gonna gitcha back to your village so a real medicine man can fix this leg up proper.

After feeding the animals all he could spare, and giving each a hat full of water, Mac grabbed his bedroll and returned to the fire. "That foot fell okay?"

"Yes! The pain is good, because I know that it is still there and will soon be ready to carry me across the land again."

"Mebbe not as soon as you want, but I reckon it's gonna be just fine 'fore too long." He shook the blanket to rid it of scorpions that might be hitching a warm ride across the desert. After holding it out and checking in the firelight that there was nothing on it, he spread it across the Apache.

After a long silence, the Apache spoke. "You are a strange white man, to be helping an Apache."

Mac finished chewing his cat before answering. "I was married to a Kawevikopaya Yavapai woman for many years, and she was the best human being that I have ever known." He remained silent then and stared into the fire…the Apache noticed the change.

"The Tonto Apache are a good people, who like my people, only ask to be left alone to live as they choose on their ancestral land." He too remained silent…sensing the white man's need to let his mind wander through the past.

Mac finally spoke…quietly…reverently, "Lost her a month ago to the disease those damn soldiers brought with 'em."

"The one that makes spots all over the body?"

"Yes!"

"It has killed more of my people than white man's bullets."

"Them bastards in Washington probably gave it to the soldiers and then sent 'em here so your people would get it and die. Then they could claim all of the land that you've been on forever."

"That is what my brother-in-law, Juh, the Chiricahua Chief has said since our people began dying with the red spots on them."

"I reckon he knows what he's talkin about." Mac chewed his last chunk of cat in silence, and when it was gone he spoke quietly with a melancholy tone to his usually boisterous voice. "I put Rainbow in the ground and sold out. Gonna go to Mexicali and try to forget how hard she died."

"I have heard of the town but never went there. You have a friend in this place?"

"Rainbow's sister married a California Mexican who has a ranch somewhere near there." Mac took a sip of water to wash down the cat, then said, "I reckon I can find him, and lay up there a while, till I figure out what to do with my final years…I'm lost without Rainbow."

The following morning, the swelling had gone down significantly, and by the next morning the Apache's leg looked good enough to begin heading toward his village—a secret camp in the Sierra Madre Mountains.

Mac helped the Apache get into Bladder's saddle, because the horse's gait was much smoother than the mule's. As they rode along he asked the Apache what had happened to his horse.

"When I am troubled, I go for long walks. I walked farther than I should have and became tired." He grinned at MacCrimmon, "I sat by the wrong boulder."

• • •

Rick Magers

At noon the next day Mac rode his mule into the Apache's camp. The man on the horse was exhausted and his leg was swollen again from hanging down beside the horse, but he smiled as his people came out to greet him yelling, jur-ahn'-i-moh, jur-ahn'-i-moh, jur-ahn'-i-moh.

Mac turned and looked at the Apache, "Well I'll be damned, so you're the great Chiricahua Chief Geronimo?"

"No, I am a Chiricahua warrior who tries to lead his people along the right path when Chief Juh is not in the camp." He reached out and offered his hand to Mac, and they clasp each other on the wrist. "You may stay in my camp as long as you want, and when you leave, I will have already sent runners to spread the word that you saved me from the buzzards." He released Mac's wrist and removed the amulet that he wore around his neck, and then passed it to Mac. "When you show this to the Chiricahua people along the way to Mexicali, they will know who you are and will help you to reach your destination safely."

• • •

MacCrimmon remained in Geronimo's camp for two weeks, so that his horse and mule could regain their strength. During that short length of time he learned that the rumors being spread about Geronimo were not true. He was simply a man who had watched his people being cheated and stolen from by the invading white men, and decided that he would try to stop it.

At one time during his quest to lead his people to a better life, he and his small band of warriors were pitted against 5,000 soldiers of the United States Army, 500 scouts, and 3,000 Mexican soldiers…still he led his handful of warriors to safety and left many foreign invaders behind him—dead.

It took Apache deserters who abandoned their people and became scouts for the army, in exchange for a few shiny coins and white man's whiskey, to discover Geronimo's hidden mountain lair.

The Chiricahua warrior finally surrendered to Gen. Nelson Miles on Sept. 4, 1886. Eight years later, after confinement in Florida, Geronimo was allowed to become a rancher near Fort Sill Oklahoma.

When President Theodore Roosevelt personally requested that he ride with him in the 1905 inaugural parade, Geronimo said that he would, if his friend who had saved his life, Glyn MacCrimmon, who was a rancher in Mexicali, was brought east so he could also ride in the parade.

Teddy Roosevelt admired men with spunk, and authorized a team of men to go to the little town that sat on the USA side of the border. A few days after arriving in Mexicali, they located a very surprised Glyn MacCrimmon, who accepted the president's offer…partly because he had never seen a real live President of the United States, and partly because he wanted to meet Geronimo again to talk about all they had done in the years since they met on the Arizona desert.

It was a momentous occasion in both men's lives, and they enjoyed talking to President Roosevelt during a luxurious banquet that was held after the parade. Both men attended the inauguration and returned to their friends with tales such as none had ever heard.

•••

On a very sad historical note, Geronimo died at age 80 on Feb. 17, 1909, still a prisoner of war, unable to return to his homeland. He was buried in the Apache cemetery at Fort Sill, Oklahoma.

Glyn MacCrimmon lived five more years and died peacefully at age 91 in his bed on the small cattle ranch that he built from scratch at age seventy-two.

THE END

Rick Magers

10

SEMINOLE

Dancing Snake was named after the anhinga, a bird that moves through the water with only its head and long neck protruding. As the bird propels its body through the water, the neck moves gracefully back and forth. To anyone who has never witnessed the bird moving through the water after a meal of small fish, it appears to be a snake dancing across the water.

With similar lithe movements, the young Seminole brave moved gracefully through the thick vegetation that thrived throughout the Everglades.

Old Panther stood beside Dancing Snake as they watched the strange ships approaching the coast of Florida. "These boats are like those described by Ossatola," he said while squinting through the thin oriental-like slits covering his eyes.

"Yes! The giant shields on the sticks catch the wind and moves the big canoes for them." Dancing Snake was in awe of the huge vessels, and could not take his eyes from them.

"We must move along the jungle with them as Ossatola and his warriors did, and observe them when they come onto the land."

The two Seminole warriors moved along the east coast of Florida, keeping watch on the Spanish ships that were scouting the new land; discovered only two decades earlier by Christopher Columbus. Few

Seminoles had ever dreamed of such ships, and fewer still had ever seen one.

• • •

Captain Emmanuel Hectare turned to his mapmaker. "Is there not one harbor along this Godforsaken coast?"

"Appears not, Captain. We have traveled many days and have not seen an anchorage suitable for even these small reconnaissance vessels."

"We must anchor off every night," Captain Hectare proclaimed, "and not miss a suitable harbor…if one exists. Admiral Gomez will have his fleet ready soon after we return to Mother Spain. We must be able to give him the information he shall need to land his troops, and find the natives who can lead him to their gold mines," he paused as his eyes scanned the coast they were approaching. "Their mines must be numerous to get so much gold for the trinkets they wear."

"I fear he shall be forced to land the men with longboats and then rendezvous with them on the western coast of this wild land. There are scattered small harbors along this coast that will allow the longboats to safely land, but it appears that there are none which will accommodate our large vessels." The mapmaker lowered his long telescope and turned to the captain, "Another option would be to land troops on the southern end of the west coast, where we found the small islands surrounded by shallow water. There are a couple of good areas where Admiral Gomez' fleet of ships could safely offload troops, and then rendezvous with them at the large harbor which our explorers discovered only a few days sailing north."

The captain scanned the coastline for a long time before speaking. "That would be an arduous trek for our soldiers, and will certainly be fraught with death and disease." The captain lowered his long glass again and shook his head, "And if troops are set ashore along this coast, only God knows what will be lurking beyond these beautiful sand beaches." He passed the glass to his aide, who was always at his elbow awaiting orders. "Put this in my cabin." Still scanning the coast, he spoke quietly; almost to himself, "We will return with your maps and information, then allow the admiral to make the decision where to go ashore."

Before Captain Hectare's small reconnaissance fleet had reached modern day Jacksonville, huge swells were rolling in from the north. The worried navigator approached the captain. "Sir, these long swells are growing taller as we speak and they offer evidence that a nor'easter is moving toward us. I suggest we put to sea and head toward home. I have talked with many who have also skirted this coast and they found no harbors either."

"Yes! I'm forced to agree with you that there are no harbors along this coast, and I too have been watching the waves coming from the north. As soon as Paul has the final sketch of this section completed for the maps, we will head toward Mother Spain."

The two Seminole warriors had moved north with the Spanish vessel for several days. They had already eaten the dried fish and fowl they had carried with them, and were now eating what they could find along the way. Dancing Snake and Old Panther watched from concealment behind giant bushes along the beach. "They did not find what they looked for," the old warrior stated, and then added with an ominous tone, "but I fear that they will return."

Dancing Snake continued watching until the sails disappeared over the eastern horizon and then mumbled, "Perhaps."

• • •

Captain Hectare waited outside the Vice Admiral's office the entire morning. He was an extremely principled man who believed fervently in dress and protocol. He sat rigidly in his full dress uniform staring at the opposite wall—refusing offers of both chilled wine and hot tea by the Vice Admiral's secretary. He heard loud voices emanating through the huge wide doors, and knew they concerned the planned voyage to New Spain.

The secretary left for lunch and asked if he would like something brought back. The captain politely refused and the man left.

An hour after the secretary returned, the doors opened and the Vice Admiral walked to the captain; who jumped to his feet and stood at attention. "Emmanuel, please come in." He held out his hand and the captain shook it. They had climbed the naval ladder together, but his childhood friend was now several rungs higher.

Inside, the Vice Admiral introduced the captain to the men who were gathered around a large round map table. He shook each man's hand as his friend introduced them.

"Delgado Rona, president of the Bank of Spain, which will be the primary financier of this exploration." The banker nodded his head briskly.

"Andre Copal, owner of the ship building yard where the vessels were constructed during the past three years." He also nodded.

"Rudolf Echiavaria, owner of Seville Iron Works where the gold will be cast into new coins for Spain." A born skeptic; he said nothing.

"Come Emmanuel and look at this map." He placed his pointer near present day Port St. Lucie. "See here at the center of New Spain, where the land breaks away and heads south as small islands." The Vice Admiral held his pointer on the spot and turned to Emmanuel.

The captain looked but kept silent a moment. Finally he turned to his friend, who was now in a position of power and could drastically alter his career in the navy. Captain Hectare reluctantly said, "Vice Admiral, sir, this map is very old and outdated, and there is nothing like that in the area you point to." There was an immediate silence in the huge room. "May I use your pointer, sir?"

The Vice Admiral was frowning as he stared at the map, but handed the pointer to the captain. Emmanuel moved it to where Miami would one day lay, and then he slowly moved it toward the beginning of the Florida Keys. "Along here sir, there are many small islands with much shallow water surrounding them." Placing the pointer where future Key Largo would be, he said, "Here is where those small islands that you mentioned begin. Between them are swift running channels that are too shallow for our vessels, so we explored them in our long boats. Unfortunately sir, there were no harbors there either where your fleet could anchor safely." He moved the pointer to Key West saying, "Here we spotted tall masts, but soon, several small ships came out and with sails full, gave chase. We have heard that there are pirates in this area somewhere, and since we were not escorted by fighting galleons, we raised all sails before the wind and easily ran away from them. I have talked to captains who ventured into the waters on the west coast of New Spain, and they claim that there is a large natural harbor along here somewhere." He ran the pointer across the Tampa area. "I plan to have that area explored in hopes of locating such a harbor, if indeed it exists."

Rick Magers

The Vice Admiral looked completely dumfounded as he absorbed the information. He had known Captain Hectare since childhood and trusted his integrity, plus he considered his friend to be one of the best captains in the Spanish Navy. The Vice Admiral turned to the other men, who also had perplexed frowns. "Gentlemen, we will have to go to our alternate plan of landing our troops by longboat, and then establishing a rendezvous point somewhere on the western coast of New Spain."

The Vice Admiral sensed a critical moment of indecision among the men involved in his plan to secure vast amounts of gold in Florida. Savages had displayed many golden trinkets and adornments to a priest who made an attempt to civilize them. The adventurous priest and his fifty-man group entered Florida, which they promptly named New Spain, from the west after crossing the Gulf of Mexico. They were aboard the very vessel whose captain told of a natural harbor on the west coast of Florida. Of the fifty-one men who entered the jungle near present day Tampa, only the priest and one man survived.

For a year the priest talked about giant lizards with teeth that snatched his men so fast, the beasts were seldom seen—snakes so deadly that death occurred within minutes after being bitten—bugs more numerous that the letters in the Bible—and gold. Bugs and beasts were quickly forgotten but the word gold mesmerizes all who hear it mentioned. The priest was soon locked away in a dungeon for the insane, but his tales of gold lingered on. "Gold," he said to any audience who would listen, "so abundant that the native children play with it until something new arises. They leave a kings ransom lying on the ground and run to play with a crooked stick. Gold, I tell you. Golden robes adorning new brides, such as the royalty of Spain have never seen. Gold woven into rope to hang from trees, as nothing more that adornment for the forest. That we might survive to bring this news to our king, we ate the flesh of our fallen comrades."

Until death relieved him of his burden, he babbled endlessly about paths of pure gold running through forests—trees a hundred meters tall which were decorated with golden trinkets, and golden ropes to pull ones self to the top of mountains made of gold nuggets. In all lands, the mere mention of gold distorts men's vision and leads them to make bizarre exaggerations never before heard.

Guards listened, dreamed of vast wealth, and repeated the priest's stories. Soon, men who should have known better were dreaming too.

Rick Magers

The Vice Admiral was one of the dreamers. He was certain that the gold was there, and that he could secure a very large portion for himself after providing a vast fortune to a government desperately low of funds.

He turned to the captain. "Emmanuel, when will your map maker have his notes transferred to the new maps he created during your trip?"

"A fortnight at the very outside sir. He works very long hours on them."

"Very well Emmanuel, bring them as soon as they are completed and we will decide where to land the troops and where to rendezvous." He turned to the boat builder, "Andre can you have two additional longboats built in time to be loaded aboard each vessel that will carry the troops?"

"Certainly sir, once we had the templates and jigs set up, we put out the other thirty-two in eleven days."

The Vice Admiral nodded appreciatively, "Very well then, I'll let you all know when the maps arrive and we'll put the finishing touches on this expedition and get it under way."

• • •

Dancing snake ran into the Seminole village of his father's friend, Neomathla. It was located in the forest near the eastern shore of Lake Okeechobee. The old chief was sitting beside a smoldering bed of coals tempering arrow shafts. He looked up at the panting young man, "What is chasing you Anhinga, a panther?" The old man began calling him Anhinga when the boy was still very young. Many now referred to him by that name, due to his uncanny ability to stalk and kill game that few could get close to…he felt honored.

"The ocean has filled with the men in strange canoes." He bent over, holding his hands on his knees as he gasped for breath.

Chief Neomathla listened as the young warrior described what he had seen during a visit to the coastal village of a friend. Old Panther stood quietly beside to the young warrior…nodding his head at times. He was breathing normal as he confirmed what the excitable young warrior had said.

The serious expression on the chief's face made it obvious that he was concerned. "Come and sit with me while my messengers listen."

He turned to the woman preparing turtle stew in the turtle's shell filled with water and simmering above a fire. "Go tell the messengers to come to my chickee."

Minutes later, five young Seminole runners climbed up onto the raised floor of the chief's palm frond thatched living quarters. Once they were seated, the chief asked Dancing Snake and Old Panther to tell the five young men what they had seen. "They are the fastest runners in my tribe and will go to the villages along this side of the land near the big lake." The chief silently looked into the distance for a moment before speaking again. "Our Medicine Man had a vision about strange men wearing clothes so hard that our arrows bounced off. They came to this land in giant canoes with wings that moved them faster than we can paddle our dugouts. Before his vision ended they were more numerous than the mosquitoes, and the sky was full of more canoes with wings."

After Dancing Snake re-told what they had seen, Old Panther added, "They will return; Medicine Woman also saw strange men in her dreams. She said they will come to take the land and make slaves of our people."

The eastern tribes of the Seminole Nation met in council to discuss the sighting of strange men entering their land, once again. It was decided that a watch would be established along the east coast, and that all of the tribes would contribute men to man the posts.

During a warm summer morning in 1713 the Seminole watch near the coastal area that would one day become Ft. Pierce, spotted sails. Word of the arrival of many giant canoes with wings was sent to every tribe along the coast, and then later to the tribes inland near Lake Okeechobee.

Admiral Gomez instructed the captains of his eight huge galleons; each carrying over a hundred handpicked soldiers—to anchor their ships and lower the six longboats. "Take advantage of this calm weather and get those troops on the beach as swiftly as possible." He then had his four smaller supply ships get in as close to the beach as possible and anchor. "Get your barges in the water and begin stacking the supplies on the beach while my carpenters construct a cover for the boxes." He then sent a message to his three livestock ships. "Move near the shore and shove the horses into the water and they will swim to land and remain nearby to feel safe."

The Seminole lookouts watched in amazement as the beach filled with strange men wearing iron clothing, and animals such as they had never seen. The Spanish horses were twice as large as the small wild marshtackie horses that some Seminole tribes captured and rode. Three days later, well-concealed Indians watched as the winged canoes flew east and disappeared—leaving the strange men, giant horses, and mountains of boxes behind.

• • •

General Antonio Loupe Alvarez had risen to his current rank without once placing his foot on a battlefield. His family's influence reached into the highest areas of government, and he was more than willing to use his many contacts to attain his goals. The orders that he gave his officers were not the result of tested war decisions, made during the many battles that were faced and won by his contemporaries, but merely his personal assessment of the current situation. He had insisted that he be allowed to accompany his troops on this quest to locate the vast resources of gold and jewels known to exist in New Spain. His position as a General in Spain's army at age twenty-six did not come with wealth or even a large paycheck. Poor investments by his family had left them all struggling to maintain their lofty positions. A promise of wealth was made to those men who would see to it that Antonio was promptly promoted to General and placed in charge of the expedition—which would determine the Alvarez family's future. He and his family were about to learn a very hard lesson concerning the value of experience when waging war on a people who were as at home in their wild terrain as the Spaniards were in their own plush gardens.

Before the sails of his fleet were beyond the eastern horizon, on their way south to rendezvous with him in sixty days somewhere near present day Miami, General Alvarez was demanding that his officers have their men ready to enter the wild land adjacent to the beach within five days…in full armor.

Rick Magers

● ● ●

The young Seminole spoke so rapidly in an excited voice that the chief had to calm him to understand what he had seen. "There are more men in shiny clothes than there are deer in our forests, and they have horses twice as large as our marshtackie, and…

The chief listened without comment as the boy talked on about the men camped on the beaches, a mere day's journey east of the camp where the chief now sat. The young warrior was born and raised within the camp, and although excitable, he was never known to exaggerate. Within the hour his people were packed and moving west toward the large lake. Runners were sent to warn the many other camps in the area to head west immediately and rendezvous at the huge Seminole camp on the eastern edge of the lake.

● ● ●

General Alvarez sat atop his white stallion and issued orders to his field commanders. Each had proven their worth in previous battles, but none had ever seen or heard of a land such as they now prepared to enter.

One soldier whispered to his friend, "Now I know why there were no saddles among the supplies that we placed on the beach."

"Yes!" His friend answered, "The horses are to carry our supplies as we walk until finding the gold mines or reach Spain again."

There would be no gold and only a few would see Spain again.

A new morning sun lit the area, as the general led over eight hundred seasoned soldiers, each in full battle armor, into the unknown wilds of Florida. Behind them came a varied assortment of support personnel. Cooks, shoemakers, armor repairmen, plus medics skilled in treating wounds, diseases, and pulling bad teeth. Following them were the general's six servants. Each tended a horse carrying fine wines that he planned to enjoy with a variety of special dried foods he brought for his private cook to prepare each night. Last were the animal tenders leading twenty huge draft horses carrying gear and supplies.

The general was warned that it would require twice that many horses to carry enough supplies to last his troops until they reached the ships. He scoffed at the idea of pampering field troops. "My soldiers are seasoned veterans who are used to doing without."

The money saved by taking half as many supply horses and animal tenders, financed the wine and special food that the general took for his personal pleasure. As it turned out however, the additional horses and supplies would not be needed.

• • •

Neomathla was chief of the largest tribe of Seminole Indians living on the lake. He was in the sixth decade of his life and had battled tribes from the west and north who had tried to invade Florida. He was respected by every chief whose tribe was in the central portion of Florida, so when he asked them to come and sit with him, they willingly came to his camp.

"Before bringing your warriors here, you have moved your old people, women, and children into the swamps where they will be safe, and left guards to assist them. I hope it will be unnecessary, but we must see what these strange men want. You have all listened as my runners spoke of what they saw, and it does not appear to be a friendly visit. We will approach them as though they are an enemy and attack if they are. Scouts watch as they approach, but they move slowly like the turtle. Our scouts have determined that we are twice as many numbers as the invaders, but they might have weapons that we have never seen. A small group of warriors will approach them tonight when they stop. If they are friendly then we will talk to them in sign to determine why they are here, but if they are not, we will defeat them as we have all other invaders."

• • •

General Alvarez was enjoying smoked sausages and a fruit wine when the young messenger came to his area. "General Sir, Captain Pessa has captured three natives and is holding them until you arrive. The general dismissed the boy and said he'd be there soon, and called his valet. "I must be in full uniform Aldo, so you can begin assembling it while I finish my dinner."

An hour later he entered the captain's tent. "I see you have the three savages securely tied to trees, Captain Pessa."

"Yessir," he said while briskly saluting.

"Have you been able to communicate with them?"

"Nossir. They seem to have no understanding of language and only grunt and make sounds like animals, so I doubt they have knowledge of language."

"While at the University of Madrid I studied sign language, which the deaf use, so perhaps I can make them understand what we are searching for. Bring your lamp and we shall see."

The general walked stiffly to the three warriors and stood motionless long enough for each to inspect the many medals on his well decorated uniform. He snapped his fingers and a servant approached with a small wooden box and held it out. The general opened it and removed a large gold nugget. Holding it in the lamp's light he signed, *we want this*. When his motions were met with silence and questioning eyes, he tried again with another approach. *Where can we find this?* The three Seminoles looked at each other and talked in their language then all shrugged their shoulders before saying in their own sign language, *we have never seen that*.

After one frustrating hour, the general told the captain to leave them tied to the trees and he would try again in the morning, before they continued toward the south.

A guard awakened the captain during the hour just prior to dawn. "Captain, captain, the savages have escaped." The captain rushed naked from his tent to see the ropes, which he'd securely tied the three savages with, lying severed upon the ground.

"I turned away from the men to accustom my eyes to the darkness of the surrounding jungle, as I did every few minutes, and when I turned back they were gone."

The general was summoned, and after ranting and raving about the captain's inept abilities as a leader of men, issued the order to move out at dawn. Mere yards away, dark eyes were watching as the long caravan headed deeper into the deadly swamps and forests of the inhospitable Florida Everglades.

Rick Magers

"We now know that these strange men are here to do us harm." Chief Neomathla looked at each chief a moment before continuing. "We have been long with no invaders and many of our best warriors have never seen battle, but if we must fight these men then it will be as it is when we hunt the opossum—easy to find and easy to kill. First we will move with them and watch, because to lose a war is never a good thing."

Captain Pessa ran ahead to catch up with the general's horse. Out of breath due to the heat and heavy steel armor he wore, the captain gasped a few times before talking. "Sir, have you noticed the savages occasionally showing themselves along the way?"

"Yes I have, and I'm certain that they are in fear of us. Did you notice two nights ago, when the three that you had for a short time as your prisoners," he glared at the captain a moment before continuing, "could not keep their eyes from the many medals on my uniform?"

"Yessir, I did."

"My guess is that they believe me to be a God sent to them, and now await my orders for them to come to me."

"Yessir, those three were obviously very impressed with you."

"Tonight when we camp I will lure some of them to me and we will not let them go until we have extracted from them the information we seek."

"Very good sir," he saluted smartly, "I will return now to my troops." Later that night he approached the general's tent, followed by two young soldiers.

"Good evening, sir. I have the items you asked for." He turned to the two men, "Place the boxes on the ground in the light of the campfire and stand by for the general's orders."

"Very well, Captain Pessa, we will now see if these savages can resist coming to see what I have brought for them. Have your men place several items in the low limbs of trees beyond the fire's light and we shall enjoy some wine as we await the savages' decision."

While still in the harbor at Seville, two trunks had been filled with inexpensive, gaudy jewelry that was of little value to anyone other than the whores who worked the waterfront. The two soldiers hung necklaces, bracelets, and decorative hair combs on bushes and tree limbs, and then hastily returned to the safety of the camp.

Rick Magers

An hour later, two young Seminole braves cautiously approached. They were wearing many of the items left beyond the firelight. Unknown to the general was that they had been instructed by their chief to approach the strangers. "Wear the strange men's gifts and go to their camp. We will watch and be ready to attack if you give the signal."

The general and the captain were drinking wine at a small, unique folding table made of lightweight imported balsa wood by Seville master craftsman, Enrique Ende. He presented it to the general as a gift prior to departure of the exploration fleet; hoping to receive favors upon the general's return.

"I believe there are natives coming, sir." The captain pointed at the two Seminole Indians emerging cautiously from the darkness.

The general placed his cut crystal glass down and stood. Making the sign for peace, he approached the two Indians. "Come let me show you the many nice things we have brought to your people."

When the Seminoles reached the box that the general was pointing at, several armed soldiers stepped from the darkness and grabbed them. A shrill whistle left the lips of both natives and pierced the darkness. Before the soldiers or their nearby officers realized that the sound was coming from the lips of the Indians, both men dropped to the ground as arrows hit the soldiers and barely missed the general and the captain. The main objective of the warriors standing ready in the darkness was the safety of their friends. They concentrated their deadly arrows toward the soldiers holding the two Indians.

As soon as arrows began striking their captors the two warriors leaped to their feet and disappeared into the darkness. A short time later, Chief Neomathla sat in a clearing with the two rescued braves and the men who shot arrows into the Spaniards. "We are now certain that these men did not come in peace, so we will let them have the land that they came for." He paused a moment then finished, "We shall let them all lie on it for eternity."

Four of the six soldiers were dead and the remaining two were seriously wounded. The general had never seen a man killed, and ran screaming into his tent as arrows began hitting the soldiers who had earlier removed their armor. The captain rushed to the aid of his men and pulled two into the darkness, and rushed to a third as arrows were still flying into the camp.

The general regained his composure and called out to the captain, "Have those savages stopped shooting at us?"

"Yessir General, the two that we held ran into the jungle and the shooting stopped moments later." Captain Julio Pessa had seen many men panic the first time they were confronted by an enemy trying to kill them—he did not hold it against the general. "I believe it's safe to come out now."

The first thing the general saw upon leaving the tent was men lying on the ground with arrows protruding from them. They were groaning as the captain moved them, so that the medic who was summoned could inspect their wounds.

Several soldiers had grabbed their weapons and rushed into the general's campsite. They now stood ready along the perimeter as they held shields with swords drawn.

Ashen faced, the general redeemed himself in the captain's eyes by asking, "What can I do to help these men?" He complied with the captain's request and kneeled to hold a dying soldier's hand while repeating, "You will be okay, Soldier." Word of his assistance spread through the ranks, and his popularity among the men soared.

Neomathla brought all of his chiefs together to plan the first attack. "These invading men, who wear clothes made of iron, have giant horses, and arrived in huge canoes with wings, are here to make slaves of us. They grabbed our men two times and would have killed them if not for the swift action of our braves." He paused and looked directly at each sub-chief before continuing. "We must lure them to the great lake, and then have warriors come behind and prevent them from fleeing, as others attack from both sides along the shoreline."

"Chief Opopkahatta," he turned to the old man sitting with him, "was victorious in many battles with the Shawnee when they came south to steal his people and make slaves of them. He is a thinking warrior who uses every bit of potential strategy to beat his enemies, and is respected by all who know him."

Chief Neomathla turned and looked again at his old friend, Chief Opopkahatta, when he spoke. "Every great battle must be controlled by a great warrior, and you are the best, so if you will lead us into this fight with the strange men, then I and all others will follow your orders."

• • •

As the Spaniards buried their four dead comrades, and medics tried in vain to save the two injured soldiers, General Gomez sat alone in his tent holding his head in both hands as he wept. *What in the world have I gotten myself into?* He had instructed his valet and servants to stay outside until called. He walked back and forth inside his personal tent, which was four times larger than any of those shared by groups of ten soldiers. Through eyes red from weeping, he stared at the large portrait attached to one of the center poles. In it he was dressed in full uniform, which was embroidered elaborately with gold thread. Thirty medals hung across the front to let everyone know that they were in the presence of a very important member of the Spanish court. Through proud eyes he stared belligerently at the artist who was hired by his mother to immortalize her son.

He returned to his seat and once again held his head in his hands. *I must not fail or mother will throw herself to her death from the walls of the castle. Oh dear God, please give me strength. Mother could never live without her maids and servants.*

"Have both men died?" Captain Pessa stared at the two soldiers lying on thin groundsheets in the medic's tent.

The medic looked up, "Nossir Captain, but they will not survive the night." One soldier opened his eyes to stare at the two men.

Before the sun was above the horizon the following day, both of the remaining soldiers had also been buried. General Alvarez had regained his composure and was in conference with Captain Pessa. "We must get our troops moving soon if we are to ever locate the source of the gold that these savages are hiding."

"I agree, sir. I will organize four groups of scouts to guard the main body as we pursue the savages. One group will precede us and another will follow. Scouts on each side at a fair distance will guard our flanks. If any of the scouts encounter the enemy, we will be close enough to hear their warning, and immediately prepare for battle."

Rick Magers

"Very good Captain, we must not be surprised by these heathens again." He turned to look at the many tents with morning fires in front, as his soldiers cooked their breakfast. "Instruct the men to be in full armor and ready to move by noon." He turned and left the captain's tent without saying another word.

Captain Pessa stared at the general and shook his head slowly. *Full armor in this heat as we trek through this unusual country will be very difficult for the men.*

Dancing Snake was near enough to hear every word spoken by the general and the captain. Although he could not understand what was being said, he could tell by the way the man who wore jewelry and rode the large white horse pointed and moved his arms, that they were instructing the warriors to prepare to move. He continued watching, as the strange chickees were taken apart and loaded upon the backs of the huge horses. Before the sun was overhead, the strange warriors wearing iron clothes moved past the young scout and headed toward the huge lake; called Okeechobee by the Seminole. He noted how many were in the forward, rear, and flank guard, and also how far out they were from the main group of soldiers.

Chief Opopkahatta listened very carefully with great interest as Anhinga explained what he had seen while observing the enemy.

"…and they have twenty soldiers in front and also to the rear, plus on each side as scouts. The soldiers are now moving, with the scouts remaining ten grown pine tree lengths from them." Chief Neomathla and the sub-chiefs remained silent and listened. When Anhinga finished, he was thanked for his willingness to remain so close to the enemy for two days and nights to gather needed information. He left the war council's chickee and joined his fellow warriors, who were making thousands of arrows.

As the reed shafts were cut to length and trimmed, they were passed to another group who attached a bone or seashell tip and then bound it tightly with thin strips of deer hide. The final stage was given to the women. With nimble fingers they applied deer hoof glue to three carefully trimmed feathers and attached them to the shaft just ahead of the notch that the bowstring would fit into.

With hundreds of Seminoles working together, the arrows were soon ready. Those who had acquired steel knives, from victims who had entered their lands in times past, sharpened them. Others were checking the bindings that held the sabers of dead enemies to wooden shafts, which would be used as lances and spears. Those who had animal bone knives were carefully scraping the blades to a sharp edge and tip.

Some of the Seminoles had encountered strange men similar to those now moving into their lands. They spread the word that these strange men were good warriors and should be taken very seriously. Describing the large horses these men used, they suggested that when possible they should kill them. "I myself have seen these men kill one of the big horses and eat it, so we should do the same when we can. Perhaps we can gain knowledge from watching these men and then use it against them."

• • •

Captain Pessa was dressed in field clothing beneath his chest armor and thought it odd that General Alvarez was wearing a dress uniform and had no armor on. In five days they had moved less than fifty miles from the coast where the transport ships had deposited them. During those few days, seven men had been bitten by rattlesnakes and died soon after. Five more had been bitten by cottonmouth moccasins and also died.

They were now entering a completely different terrain as they neared the huge lake, which they had read about in the journal from the only previous expedition. As they approached a point a few miles south of the present day town of Okeechobee, the firm ground that they had felt beneath their feet was turning into water covered marsh with tall dry grass as far as they could see. Smaller trees had replaced the large trees along the coast, and bushes that sat isolated on small hammocks were long distances apart.

Two servants were exhausted and falling behind the main army. Their water-filled goatskin canteens were empty by noon, and when they saw a small lake that the soldiers were skirting, they rushed to it for a drink and to re-fill their canteens. Both men soon had their heads beneath the surface and were vigorously scrubbing their bug-infested hair.

Two bulging eyes appeared just above the surface; two feet behind two small nostrils feeding air to a hideous, prehistoric creature that had changed little since dinosaurs walked the earth. It watched the men as its long scaly tail slithered silently back and forth beneath the surface. A hunting companion silently moved through the water beside it. In the time required for the two servants to cool their heads and fill the canteens, the two 14 foot long alligators had moved unseen to within striking distance.

When the two creatures lunged from the water, their tooth-lined jaws were held wide open. Their long powerful tails easily provided the momentum necessary for the beasts to come halfway out of the water as each grabbed a different man. So swift was their action that their brief screams were unheard by the main army, now a hundred yards ahead…unaware that they were entering an area where they would be seen as either a food source or an enemy.

The Spaniards moved slowly ahead as their scouts signaled that the way ahead was clear. Lying within a few feet of the scouts were Seminole warriors watching every move the Spaniards made. Chief Opopkahatta's scouts had accumulated valuable information that would be used defeat the Spaniards.

• • •

Gray Panther approached the fire where his chief sat with other sub-chiefs, discussing their strategy to attack the strange warriors the following day. He stood patiently awaiting his chief's summoning. "Gray Panther, come and tell us what you have learned."

"Yes my chief." He nodded respectfully to each of the sub-chiefs, acknowledging their authority over him. "The one who wears no iron clothes and rides the huge white horse is not a demon who cannot be hurt. He is slapping at mosquitoes so much that he will not be able to fight, because his arms will be too tired to lift his long knife." They all chuckled at the young boy's sense of humor. "The warriors are quietly removing small pieces of their iron clothes and dropping them, so they can scratch the places where the mosquitoes have bitten. I think if we allow two more days to pass, they will all have removed their iron clothes and then our arrows will find flesh to burrow into."

Chief Opopkahatta nodded toward his nephew, Gray Panther, "You have done a very good job. We will discuss your suggestion. Now go to your fire and enjoy some delicious opossum and cabbage that your mother made, and tell her that we thank her for sending us some; we all enjoyed it very much."

• • •

"**Captain Pessa.**" The General's voice was apprehensive.

"Yessir." The captain turned toward General Alvarez who was sitting opposite him sipping wine.

"Are those fires of the savages as close as they seem?"

"I hope not, sir. I believe this clear night air makes it seem so; they are no doubt far away. They would not so brazenly flaunt their location if they were close."

The fires were, in fact, merely decoy fires a short distance away to worry the Spaniards, set purposely and tended by one warrior. The main body of Seminole had left the area and moved to a point half way to Lake Okeechobee.

Chief Opopkahatta had decided to use Gray Panther's advice and let the Spaniards suffer with their steel armor two more days before attacking them. His sub-chiefs listened as he outlined his plan. "We will attack them on the third morning as they come from their sleeping place. Most will have thrown away their iron protection and will be tired after sleeping two nights on wet grass. We will move into position as silent as the alligator to strike swiftly like the rattlesnake, and then depart before they can rally. They will follow as we lead them to the big lake. We have something that they want, although I do not know what that could be, but it will be easy to lead them into a trap from which few will survive. We must take care to let a few live so they can continue to the boats with wings and tell their people what happened." He looked from one sub-chief to the next and saw, by the nodding of heads that they all agreed. One spoke, "You are wise, Opopkahatta, because others will listen to their stories and not want to return here for whatever it is they want."

• • •

The Spaniards stopped after one day of travel, and fifty servants cut bundles of sawgrass to create a soft dry area for General Alvarez to have his tent erected above. Two hours later they returned to their regular duties with bleeding arms and hands from the sharp edges of the grass. The regular soldiers were so exhausted from struggling through the tall sawgrass, and the ever-present mosquitoes, that they pulled a small bunch of grass down without even cutting it and dropped exhausted upon it. The few who had refused to discard their armor now did so and dug at their many mosquito bites until they bled.

Morning sunlight shined down upon a very tired and wet battalion of Spanish infantry. Their breakfast was sparse because the majority of servants were required to attend to General Alvarez' needs before tending to any other duties. The soldiers sat in disgruntled groups smoking cigars and chewing soggy tasteless biscuits and then washing the mess down with Troops Wine, a fermented concoction that was barely beyond a child's sweet berry juice.

It was 10:00 AM before the general was prepared to move. His breakfast had consisted of salted fish that had been dried and packed specifically for him. His personal cook arose long before dawn to put the fish in water to soak as he made fresh bread and baked it in a small folding tin oven. One of the general's many cheeses was carefully scraped to remove mold and placed on his table. A bottle of sweet wine was opened only moments prior to awakening the general.

Captain Pessa arrived each morning to dine with the general. Even though he felt bad about the conditions that his men were enduring, he never the less enjoyed beginning his day with dried meat, fresh bread, cheese, and good wine.

By noon, the Spaniards had seen nothing of the enemy, although Seminole scouts were always but a short distance away. By nightfall, the soldiers were too exhausted from the intense heat, lack of adequate food, and the ever-present mosquitoes, to bother with pulling down grass to create a better sleeping area. They lay on their back in the marsh beneath their floorless tents chewing moldy biscuits and drinking their disgusting Troops Wine…as mosquitoes dined on their blood. They awoke on the second morning exhausted and hungry, but could think of little but the dark clouds of swarming mosquitoes that seemed to fill the entire land that they had entered only days earlier. By the end of the second day not one soldier was wearing armor.

At the head of the long line of troops sat General Antonio Loupe Alvarez. Mounted on his magnificent white stallion he was an impressive figure for his men to follow, although even the men at the front of the line paid no attention to him. The general had learned, as had his troops, that the more clothing a person wore, the fewer areas of the body were available to the mosquitoes. He had wrapped a silk scarf around his entire head, but could still see ahead as he led his troops deeper into the trap ahead.

Behind the general trudged over eight hundred men. Most were once-proud soldiers who wore their armor belligerently in the face of all previous enemies, but were now clothed in a variety of garments in an effort to combat an enemy such as they had never seen…which so completely covered their flesh, that it appeared to be a moving black mass. Many had smeared mud on all exposed areas of their skin, and carried their shields and lances in hands at the end of exhausted arms hanging down at their side.

At the end of the second day that Chief Opopkahatta had given them, the long line of soldiers moved slowly into the area selected as their camp for the night. Once again they lay in wet filthy clothing and chewed soggy biscuits and ate moldy cheese. Many refused to hold up their tin cup for a ration of Troops Wine—such was their exhaustion. Some even refused their biscuit and cheese; preferring to simply rest.

It mattered little—this was to be the last night for most of them. Unheard and unseen, the Seminole warriors crept to within arrow range as the Spaniards slept. Each group awaited the coming day…one with dread…the other with glee.

• • •

When the sun began to rise above the horizon, it provided enough light to allow the Seminole braves to see the sleepy-eyed Spaniards as they shuffled tiredly from their tents. The Indians had watched for two days, and knew that the men would soon crowd around the morning fire, to be free from the incessant mosquitoes for a short time before beginning another day on the edge of the Everglades. Many years earlier, the ancestors of these natives had made their homes in the swamps of Florida in order to be free from invasion. They learned to cope with all of the living creatures that were there when they arrived. A combination of garb, diet, and natural lotions shielded them from the bugs, as knowledge protected them from the many deadly animals and vipers that shared the land with them.

The Seminole's ability to advance very close to their prey meant that they did not need long bows or arrows. As they watched the tired soldiers gather around the fire, a handful of short arrows had been shoved into the sandy bottom at their feet. They had earlier notched an arrow and now they awaited a signal from their chief.

A trilling sound blended so perfectly with the morning birds that only the 200 Seminole warriors lying in the tall grass twenty feet from the enemy heard it. Each warrior tensed and drew back the string holding a short deadly arrow.

When the prearranged signal was given, two things happened simultaneously. The warriors near the main camp stood and began firing arrows into the Spaniards who were gathered around the many morning fires. During this time, arrows were also shot into the horses tethered to a long rope between two poles. Within minutes there were over three hundred dead or dying soldiers and not one horse was standing; including the general's white stallion. As the soldiers were running around in search of their weapons, the Seminole warriors ducked back down in the tall grass and were running toward the lake. The warriors who had been given the task of killing all of the horses were the best archers in the tribe. They did not get too close for fear the horses would sense danger and spook. When all of the horses were down, the warriors were swiftly moving away from the battlefield. Once they were too far away to be seen, they too headed toward the lake to rendezvous with their comrades.

Three hundred Seminole warriors under the command of the fearless War Chief Halpatter Tustenuggee now moved into position near the dead horses to prevent the Spaniards from removing the packs of supplies that had already been strapped to the horses, in preparation for the day's march.

The Spaniards were an extremely well trained company and knew immediately what to do when the bugles bellowed their signals. More than a hundred soldiers armed with lances surrounded the area where the general and his officer's tents were set up. Each soldier held his shield high; knowing that there was no longer armor to stop the arrows.

Before the moaning of the dying had subsided, Captain Pessa turned to the general. "Sir, I believe the savages have retreated to prepare for another attack." Before the general could reply, a young messenger ran into the general's command post. The captain turned to the boy, "What is it, Renaldo?"

"Sir, the horses have all been killed."

General Alvarez turned abruptly to stare at the youth then turned his gaze toward the horse compound. "My stallion?"

The boy lowered his eyes as he answered, "Yessir, the beautiful white stallion also."

"Captain!"

Captain Pessa turned to face his commander. "Yes, general."

"We must not lose the supplies. Have men leave their weapons behind and carry those supply packs to the center of our camp."

"Yessir." The captain sent the boy messenger to his lieutenants with instructions to repeat the order just given by General Alvarez. Captain Pessa gathered two-dozen men along his route to the horse compound. They obediently shoved their lances and swords into the soft soil so they would not be weighted down, and could carry the bulky supply packs.

The weaponless Spaniards and the Seminole warriors, who were moving in from the rear, arrived at the dead horses simultaneously. Halpatter Tustenuggee had been told by Chief Opopkahatta not to allow the enemy to gather their supplies from the dead horses.

Before the Spaniards had time to remove the supply packs from the horses, arrows began dropping the defenseless men. When the soldiers saw their comrades writhing in agony at their feet, they turned and ran. Seeing the situation as hopeless, Captain Pessa also turned and began a cautious retreat.

Seminole scouts had been given instructions when the strange men first entered the Everglades. "Watch closely and determine which men are the chiefs, so that our warriors can kill them first, and the others will be easily defeated."

Before Captain Pessa had taken but a few steps, he was struck in the neck by an arrow. He held his sword in his left hand and gripped the arrow's shaft with the other. Two arrows struck him in the stomach but he stood erect and snapped the feathered end of the shaft that was protruding from his neck. As arrows began hitting him, the captain switched the sword to his right hand and gripped the end of the shaft with the portion of the shell point still attached. As he pulled the shaft on through his neck several arrows hit him in the chest. He fell back with the broken shaft still gripped in his sword hand. After dropping the bloody shaft, Captain Pessa transferred his sword to his left hand and began a courageous attempt to stand and do battle with his enemy.

A loud command by a Seminole Sub-chief halted more arrows from being shot into the captain. He made it to one knee but could go no further. His troops had abandoned him, so he remained on one knee with his sword raised toward the enemy. Blood ran freely from the wound in his neck, and his tunic was rapidly turning red. He tried in vain to focus his eyes so he could see the man approaching him.

Silent Lion approached Captain Pessa and spoke to him loud enough for his warriors to hear. "You are a brave warrior and have faced death proudly. I will tell our people of your bravery. The story will remain forever in our camps; you will never be forgotten."

The sun began setting for Captain Pessa as the enemy around him began chanting. His grip on the hilt of his sword weakened, and soon he was lying on his side. As darkness swarmed over him, he wondered if his troops were okay.

Silent Lion gave a signal and all of his warriors began moving cautiously toward the Spaniards; now gathered in the center of their encampment. Another signal from Silent Lion and two hundred Seminole women stood and began pulling fifty dugout canoes across the wet grass toward the dead horses. The flat-bottom canoes glided easily across the marsh. As Silent Lion's warriors stood guard between the Spaniards and them, the women began cutting away the packs. Once the packs were loaded into canoes, the women began butchering the horses.

Before the Spaniards had time to re-organize their defense, the canoes had once again silently disappeared into the surrounding land—inhospitable to invaders…home to the Seminole. Horsehides filled with fresh meat would be distributed to various tribes, and the supplies, even though alien to the Seminole Indians, would be met by eager hands.

• • •

When General Alvarez was told that Captain Pessa was dead, he immediately promoted Lieutenant Juan Bolar to Captain Juan Bolar. The shock of first battle had worn off and the general was at last becoming a true field commander. He listened intently when his new captain spoke. "General, I have seen twenty-seven officers with as many as a dozen arrows in them. Each was wearing his officer's tunic, which leads me to think that with so many arrows in them they were singled out as the leaders of this expedition." The general looked intently at his captain, who finally spoke again. "Sir, I would recommend that you remove your uniform jacket so you will be less conspicuous to the enemy." He paused momentarily to allow the general to absorb what he had said. "Sir!" The general turned back to him.

"Yes?"

"These soldiers have never needed a leader more than they now do." He refrained from saluting and told the general that he must see to his men. After the newly appointed captain had gone, General Alvarez looked out across the vast swamp but saw no sign of the savages, who but a short time earlier had decimated his battalion of seasoned troops. He re-entered his tent to find his servant keeping the bugs from his general's breakfast. The general placed his hand on the shoulder of the old man who had been serving the Alvarez family since a young buy. "Aldo, I have a very difficult task for you."

"Whatever you wish, sir, I will do my very best." Half an hour later the general was wearing a common soldier's tunic. His servant spoke again, "You are still their general, sir."

"Thank you, Aldo."

"I located six that will fit you, and at first opportunity I will wash the blood from them."

"Thank you, Aldo, but no. If I am to lead these men from this nightmare I must remain alive, and to do that I must appear as a common soldier in soiled garb." He gathered his remaining field officers and was shocked to learn that only eleven had survived. He promoted ten soldiers, recommended by his remaining officers, to the rank of lieutenant, and instructed the eleven remaining lieutenants to locate tunics among the dead infantrymen and discard their officer clothing.

"We must rely on God for His help against these savages, but we must also use the skills we have learned as soldiers to successfully complete our mission." He turned to look in the direction that the Seminoles had run into the swamp. "I believe we are confronting a very small band of savages, so if we maintain strict military discipline we should be able to easily defeat them, now that we have some understanding of their methods of combat." Although he spoke with confidence, General Alvarez was severely shaken by the loss of so many of his troops. His mind was in turmoil...*I wonder if we are not confronting a very large band of savages, and they are simply not letting us see their numbers?*

He would soon have his answer.

• • •

Chief Opopkahatta instructed his sub-chiefs to gather at his chickee to discuss the next stage of attack against the invaders. It took little time for the warriors to agree that the initial plan was working, and that they would continue as Chief Opopkahatta had originally ordered. War Chief Halpatter Tustenuggee's 300 warriors were behind the Spaniards and would begin setting fire to the sawgrass as soon as the signal came. Chief Alligator's 200 warriors were on the north side of the enemy and Chief Bobcat's 200 warriors were on the south side.

Chief Neomathla and his 100 warriors would tease the Spaniards into following them to the shores of Lake Okeechobee.

Chief Ohanahana's 500 warriors, which he had brought from the west side of the lake, were in dugout canoes concealed along the eastern shore, and would attack the Spaniards as soon as they were forced to the water's edge.

Chief Opopkahatta nodded his head and clapped his hands together once. "When the sun returns to the dark land tomorrow there will be only a few of the strange men left alive to return to their home and tell the story."

• • •

General Alvarez was proving to be a good leader of men. His lack of military experience was offset by his intuitive sense of well being for his men; who now looked to him for instructions. "The men on the outer perimeter of our army must at all times keep their shields up to prevent arrows from striking fatal blows on their body, and carry their sword in hand so that they can strike out instantly if these savages rise up suddenly nearby and attack in force. If that happens, you men inside must separate at the center and support the men being attacked. Those of you remaining must watch for an attack on the other side and lend support to those men on the outer boundary of that side. It is very important that those of you, both soldiers and servants, continuously be looking for the savages to attack from the rear. If that happens then you soldiers in the middle must separate at a center point running from side-to-side. Those in the rear half must defend the main body while all others remain in position and guard the left and right flank. We must never allow these savages to separate our main body into smaller groups." He looked hard at Captain Bolar, who was now Major Bolar, and his eleven seasoned lieutenants who had been promoted to captain, and then spoke to the group of newly commissioned lieutenants. "You men were recommended for promotion by your own officers, because you have proven to be courageous soldiers in battle. You must now look to the safety of these men who you fought beside in battles past, and if you do, then we shall all see Mother Spain again. Do not," the general turned his gaze to each officer before continuing, "under any circumstances allow this battalion to be separated into small groups of soldiers, or we are all doomed to remain in this Godforsaken country forever." He turned then to a small round man in a black robe. "Friar Mo Donza will now lead us in prayer."

Before the Friar began the prayer, a soldier yelled, "Look." He was pointing to smoke rising along a mile of dry sawgrass directly behind them.

With no hesitation whatsoever, General Alvarez motioned the Friar away, and instructed his new major to have his officers get the men into marching formation.

• • •

Chief Neomathla's warriors moved toward the northeastern shore of Lake Okeechobee, but made certain that the Spaniards occasionally got a glimpse of them. The general had issued orders to fire at the Seminoles only when they were within range, but after the first volley, the Indians kept just beyond the range of the Spaniard's lead shot.

So intense on the pursuit was the general that he never realized he was being drawn into an ambush. His newfound courage, leading men against the enemy as a battlefield commander, had overridden all textbook knowledge of war, which he had studied since childhood. In his mind's-eye he envisioned himself returning to Spain with tales of his courageous attacks against the savages in New Spain. He also saw himself standing next to a pile of gold such as the civilized world had never seen.

Chief Opopkahatta had carefully been watching everything and finally determined which of the strange men was the main chief. He summoned Chief Neomathla and pointed out the general. "This man is consulted by the others and he points to where he wants them to go. He must die."

General Antonio Loupe Alvarez had his ornate sword in hand and was marching forward toward his fate when several arrows hit him from both flanks. He wallowed in the tall grass until he was a muddy, bloody, ball of flailing arms. His screams went beyond his troops to be heard by every Seminole warrior.
When the Spaniards saw the flames moving swiftly toward them from the rear, they increased their speed.
Once the rear fires were burning fiercely, and riding the wind toward the Spaniards, Chief Halpatter Tustenuggee instructed his warriors to run ahead and start fires on each flank of the enemy.

The Spaniards were running west as the fires closed in on them. They reached the water, only to see Chief Ohanahana's 500 warriors appear in long dugout canoes from the shoreline grass as though by magic. The slaughter of all but a few Spaniards took less than an hour. A few warriors were killed by musket fire, and a few were wounded when they left the canoes and rushed at the Spaniards to engage them in hand-to-hand combat. Many of the Spaniards were burned to death because they were prevented from moving ahead. As the soldiers were slain, others rushed over them to escape the flames—only to be cut down by arrows, lances, knives, and war clubs. When the fast moving grass fires died in the water of Lake Okeechobee, there were still a few Spaniards aflame and running back the way they had come.
Great care had been taken to allow several of the Spaniards to escape. Unknown to them, two dugout canoes with dried food inside had been placed along the southern shore, where they had been herded

toward. The Seminole warriors fired arrows over them and screamed unintelligible threats as the men ran through the grass.

• • •

Captain Juan Bolar was one of the eleven lucky soldiers to see Spain again. He took charge of both dugout canoes, and with great skill, led his men west on the Caloosahatchee River to what would one day be Fort Myers Beach, and then north up the coast to Tampa Bay. They constructed a camp and remained there for sixty-seven days, until two Spanish vessels arrived. The captains of the vessels hoped to find General Antonio Loupe Alvarez, his army, and thousands of savages carrying bags of gold nuggets.

The Seminole Indians lived on the Florida land unmolested until white settlers determined that the land could be made to grow vegetables and fruits.

When cattlemen arrived and began creating huge herds, the Seminoles moved deeper into the wild Everglades. Land barons soon arrived and wanted even that land, and the Native American Seminole was forced to live on smaller and smaller chunks of land at the edge of millions of acres on which only the Seminole could once live and prosper.

• • •

The Seminole Indians who tourists see living in Florida today never signed a peace treaty with the United States. They are not at war with the US Government, but have never felt, and never will, that there will ever be a monetary figure that can justify what was done to them as a people—the first true North Americans.

THE END

Rick Magers

Other books

By

Rick Magers

THE McKANNAHS
~ western novel ~

DARK CARIBBEAN
~ novel based on a true story ~

LADYBUG and the DRAGON
~ biography—**FREE** as long as they last at www.grizzlybookz.com ~
Book II available soon
Follow Katia's progress against the leukemia Dragon
http://caringbridge.org/fl/katia_leukemiapage

THE FACE PAINTER
~ short stories for young readers ~

A VERY UNUSUAL COLLECTION
~ of 80 short stories ~

2 BOOKS IN 1
~ 2 dark novellas in 1 frightening book ~

Rick Magers

IN PROGRESS

THE McKANNAHS
~ together again ~

Four McKannah brothers arrive to help Jesse *right a wrong,* done to his Native American friends. Corrupt Politicians and others will wish they'd never heard of The McKannahs.

Their hair now has gray streaks running through it.

Steel gray
~ The same color as the steel running through their bodies ~

• • •

ASHES and MEMORIES
~ biography ~

• • •

CARIB INDIAN
~ warrior / cannibal ~

The first novel ever written about these ferocious South American Indians who ruled the Caribbean Sea for centuries.

Rick Magers

Available in 2007

WE HOPE

• • •

The biography of Dolores (DEO) Fisher…

widow of the author's friend; world famous treasure diver

Mel Fisher.

Many years prior to locating the $400,000,000. sunken treasure of the Spanish Galleon Atocha, not far from Key West Florida, Mel would have been the first to say that the greatest treasure he ever found was in California…it was

DEO

Together they roamed the world in search of adventure and sunken treasure…they found plenty of both.

BUT

With the many books written, a feature film, and numerous TV specials…this will be an untold side of the story. Stunning, movie star beautiful, Dolores was not window dressing…she was a full time diver who went down through the sharks like all the rest…often bringing up treasure.

Check www.grizzlybookz.com to see when it's available.

Rick Magers

BOOKS BY

RICK MAGERS

ARE AVAILABLE AT:

Amazon.com
Borders.com
Target.com
Waldenbooks.com
Alibris.com
Abebooks.com
BooksInPrint.com
GlobalBooksInPrint.com